Dear Reader,

In 2008 we adopted a two-year-old Norwegian Elkhound named Chaos. She was a retired champion show dog who had recently had a litter of puppies.

Her pedigree didn't matter to us. We didn't even bother changing the ownership on her AKC papers. All we knew was that we'd found the perfect dog for us! It was love at first sight!

My oldest daughter decided to join our county's 4-H dog programme. Soon she was doing obedience and showmanship fun matches with Chaos and loving every minute of it. She decided she wanted to try AKC Junior Handler. I knew nothing about dog showing except what I'd seen in the movie *Best In Show.* Turns out that's not too far from the truth!

Many of our weekends are now spent at dog shows. Two of my children now compete in the Juniors' ring, as well as in the Breed ring. I always take my laptop so I can write in between events. I happened to be at a dog show when I came up with the idea for this book.

I wanted to explore the idea of a heroine from the wrong side of the tracks with the ultimate good-guy hero and toss in a few dogs—both purebreds and rescues—for fun! This book was the result.

I hope you enjoy reading about Becca and Caleb and all of the pups!

Melissa

"You're the kind of guy who plays by the rules."

"Normally, yes." He moved closer. "But this isn't normal."

Becca agreed with him. She fought the urge to step back. "Being here?"

Caleb stopped in front of her, only inches away. "Being here with you. I'm tired of playing by the rules."

Her heart slammed against her ribs. She should step back. Way back. Put distance between them. For her own good.

But her feet wouldn't move. She remained rooted to the spot, waiting, hoping, anticipating.

He lowered his mouth to hers and kissed her. Hard.

Becca had never known what it was like to be possessed, but she felt possessed by Caleb's kiss. She didn't mind one bit.

THE MAN BEHIND
THE PINSTRIPES

BY
MELISSA McCLONE

First published in Great Britain 2013
by Mills & Boon, an imprint of Harlequin (UK) Limited.
Harlequin (UK) Limited, Eton House, 18-24 Paradise Road,
Richmond, Surrey TW9 1SR

© Melissa Martinez McClone 2013

ISBN: 978 0 263 23493 0

Harlequin (UK) policy is to use papers that are natural, renewable and recyclable products and made from wood grown in sustainable forests. The logging and manufacturing process conform to the legal environmental regulations of the country of origin.

Printed and bound in Great Britain
by CPI Antony Rowe, Chippenham, Wiltshire

With a degree in mechanical engineering from Stanford University, the last thing **Melissa McClone** ever thought she would be doing was writing romance novels. But analysing engines for a major US airline just couldn't compete with her 'happily-ever-afters'. When she isn't writing, caring for her three young children or doing laundry, Melissa loves to curl up on the couch with a cup of tea, her cats and a good book. She enjoys watching home decorating shows to get ideas for her house—a 1939 cottage that is *slowly* being renovated. Melissa lives in Lake Oswego, Oregon, with her own real-life hero husband, two daughters, a son, two lovable but oh-so-spoiled indoor cats, and a no-longer-stray outdoor kitty that has decided to call the garage home.

Melissa loves to hear from her readers. You can write to her at PO Box 63, Lake Oswego, OR 97034, USA, or contact her via her website: www.melissamcclone.com

Books by Melissa McClone:

WINNING BACK HIS WIFE
HIS LARKVILLE CINDERELLA*
IT STARTED WITH A CRUSH...
FIREFIGHTER UNDER THE MISTLETOE
NOT-SO-PERFECT PRINCESS
EXPECTING ROYAL TWINS!

*Part of *The Larkville Legacy* series

**Other titles by this author are available in eBook format.
Visit www.millsandboon.co.uk**

To Jan Herinckx for introducing us to
Chaos and the world of dog-showing!

Special thanks to: Terri Reed, Jennifer Shirk, Jennifer Short.
And the Immersion Crew: Margie Lawson,
Elizabeth Cockle and Lori Freeland.

CHAPTER ONE

THE INCESSANT BARKING from the backyard of his family's palatial estate confirmed Caleb Fairchild's fear. His grandmother had gone to the dogs.

Cursing under his breath, he pressed the doorbell.

A symphony of chimes filled the air, drowning out the irritating barks. Forget Mozart. Forget Bach. Only a commissioned piece from a respected New York composer would do for Gertrude Fairchild, his grandmother who had founded a billion-dollar skin care company with his late grandfather in Boise, Idaho.

Caleb was here to put an end to her frivolous infatuation with man's best friend. It was the only way to keep Fair Face, the family company, successful and profitable.

The front door opened, greeting him with a blast of cold air and a whiff of his grandmother's floral scent perfume.

Grams.

Short white curls bounced every which way. She looked fifty-seven not seventy-seven, thanks to decades of using her own skin care products.

"Caleb! I saw your car on the security camera so told Mrs. Harrison I would answer the door." The words rushed from Grams's mouth faster than lobster tails disappeared from the buffet table at the country club. "What are you doing here? Your assistant said you didn't have any free time this week. That's why I mailed you the dog care prototypes."

He hadn't expected Grams to be so excited by his visit. He kissed her cheek. "I'm never too busy for you."

Her cornflower blue eyes danced with laughter. "This is such a lovely surprise."

Sweat trickled down his back. Too bad he couldn't blame the perspiration on the warm June day.

He adjusted his yellow tie then smoothed his suit jacket. But no matter how professional he looked, she wasn't going to like what he had to say. "I'm not here as your grandson. I need to speak with you as Fair Face's CEO."

"Oh, sweetheart." The warmth in her voice added to his discomfort. "I raised you. You'll always be my grandson first."

Her words hit him like a sucker-punch. He owed Grams... everything.

She opened the door wider. "Come in."

"Nice sari," he said.

Grams struck a pose. "Just something I had in my closet."

He entered the foyer. "Better add Bollywood to your bucket list."

"Already have." She closed the door. "Let's go out on the patio and chat."

Chat, not speak or discuss or talk. Not good.

Caleb glanced around. Something was...off.

Museum-worthy works of art hung in the same places. The squeaky dog toys and ravaged stuffed animals on the shiny hardwood floor were new. But the one display he expected to see, what he wanted to see, what he longed to see was missing from its usual spot.

His throat tightened. "Where are the—"

"In the living room."

Caleb walked around the corner and saw the three-foot U.S. Navy aircraft carrier replicas showcased on a brand-new wooden display case. He touched the deck of the USS *Ronald Reagan*.

Familiar. Soothing. Home.

"I've been making some changes around here," Grams said

from behind him. "I thought they deserved a nicer place than the foyer."

He faced her. "Gramps would like this."

"That's what I thought, too. Have you eaten lunch?"

"I grabbed something on my way over."

"Then you need dessert. I have cake. Made it myself." She touched Caleb's arm with her thin, vein-covered hand. "Carrot, not chocolate, but still tasty."

Grams always felt the urge to feed him. He knew she wouldn't give up until he agreed to have a bite to eat. "I'll have something before I leave."

A satisfied smile graced her glossed lips.

At least one of them was happy.

Back in the foyer, he kicked a tennis ball with his foot. "It's a miracle you don't break a hip with all these dog toys laying around."

"I might be old, but I'm still spry." His grandmother's gaze softened. She placed her hand over her heart. "Heavens. Every time I see you, you remind me more and more of your father. God rest his soul."

Caleb's stomach churned as if he'd eaten one too many spicy Buffalo wings. He strived hard to be nothing like his feckless father. A man who'd wanted nothing to do with Fair Face. A man who'd blown through money like a hedge fund manager's mistress. A man who'd died in a fiery speedboat crash off the Cote d'Azur with his girlfriend du jour.

Grams' gaze ran the length of Caleb. She clucked her tongue. "But you've got to stop dressing like a high-class mortician."

"Not this again." Caleb raised his chin, undaunted, and followed her out of the foyer. "You'd have me dress like a rugged, action-adventure movie star. A shirtless one, given the pictures you share on Facebook."

They walked by the dining room where two elaborate chandeliers hung above a hand-carved mahogany table that sat twenty.

"You're a handsome man," Grams said. "Show off your assets."

"I'm the CEO. I have a professional image to maintain."

"There's no corporate policy that says your hair can't touch your collar."

"The cut suits my position."

"Your *suits* are a whole other matter." She pointed at his chest. "Your tie is too understated. Red screams power. We'll go shopping. Girls these days are looking for the whole package. That includes having stylish hair and being a snazzy dresser."

And not taking your grandmother's fashion advice.

They walked into the kitchen. A basket of fruit and a covered cake stand sat on the marble counter. Something simmered on the stove. The scent of basil filled the air. Normal, everyday things, but this visit home felt anything but normal.

"Women only care about the balance in my bank account," he said.

"Some. Not all." She stopped, squeezed his hand, the way she'd done for as long as Caleb remembered. Her tender touch and her warm hugs had seen him through death, heartbreak and everyday life. "You'll find a woman who cares only about you."

Difficult to do when he wasn't looking, but he wasn't telling Grams that today. One piece of bad news a day met her quota. "I like being single."

"You must have one-night stands or friends with benefits."

He flinched. "You're spending too much time on Facebook."

A disturbing realization formed in his mind. Discussing sex might be easier than talking to Grams about her dog skin care products.

She placed her hands on her hips. "I would like great grandchildren one of these years while I can still get on the floor and play with them. Why do you think I created that line of organic baby products?"

"Everyone at the company knows you want great grandchildren."

"What's a woman to do?" She put her palms up. Gold brace-lets clinked against each other. "You and your sister are in no rush to give me grandbabies while I'm still breathing."

"Can you imagine Courtney as a mom?"

"She has some growing up to do," Grams admitted, but without any accusation or disappointment. She walked into the family room with its leather couches, huge television and enough books on the floor-to-ceiling bookshelves to start a li-brary. "Though I give you credit for at least proposing to that money-grubbing floozy, Cash-andra."

Unwelcome memories flooded him. His heart cried foul. Cheat. Sucker. "Cassandra."

The woman had introduced herself to him at a benefit din-ner. Smart and sexy as hell, Cassandra knew what buttons to push to become the center of his universe. She'd made him feel more like a warrior than a businessman. Marriage hadn't been on his radar screen, but when she gave him an ultimatum, he'd played right into her hand with a romantic proposal and a stun-ning three-carat engagement ring only to find out everything about her and their relationship had been a scam, a ruse, a lie.

"Cash-andra fits." Grams held up three fingers. "Refusing to sign the agreed-upon prenup. Two-timing you. Hiring a divorce attorney before saying I do. No wonder you're afraid to date."

He squared his shoulders. "I'm not afraid."

Not afraid of Cassandra.

Not afraid of any woman.

But he was…cautious.

After Cassandra wouldn't sign the prenup, he'd called off the wedding and broken up with her. She'd begged him for a second chance, and he'd been tempted to reconcile, until a pri-vate investigator proved the woman was a gold digger in the same league as his own mother.

Grams waved a hand in the air, as if she could brush aside bad things in the world. Light reflected off her three diamond rings, anniversary presents from his grandfather. "I shouldn't have mentioned the Jezebel."

At least Caleb had gotten away relatively unscathed except for a bruised ego and broken heart. Unlike his father who'd wound up with two kids he'd never wanted.

She exited the house through the family room's French doors.

Caleb followed her outside to see new furniture—a large gleaming, teak table surrounded matching wood chairs, a hammock and padded loungers.

The sun beat down. He pulled out a chair for his grandmother, who sat. "It's hot. Let me put up the umbrella."

Grams picked up a black rectangular remote from the table. "I've got it."

She pressed a button.

A cantilevered umbrella opened, covering them in shade.

He joined her at the table.

"What do you think about the dog products?" Gertie asked.

No birds chirped. Even the crickets seemed to be napping. The only thing he heard was an occasional bark and his grandfather's voice.

Do what must be done. For Fair Face. For your grandmother.

Caleb would rather be back in his office dealing with end-of-quarter results. Who was he kidding? He'd rather be anywhere else right now.

"Interesting prototypes," he said. "Appealing fragrance and texture."

Gertie whistled. "Wait until you see them in action."

Dogs ran full speed from around the corner. A blur of gray, brown and black. The three animals stopped at Grams's feet, mouths panting and tails wagging.

"Feel how soft they are." Pride filled her voice as if the dogs were as much a part of her gene pool as Caleb was.

He rested his hands on the table, not about to touch one of her animals. "Most fur is soft if a dog is clean."

"Not Dozer's." She scooped up the little brown dog, whose right eye had been sewn shut. Not one of her expensive show dogs. A rescue or foster. "His hair was bristly and dry with flakes."

"Doggy dandruff?"

"Allergies. Animals have sensitivities like humans. That's why companies need to use natural and organic ingredients. No nasty chemicals or additives. Look at Dozer now." She stared at the dog with the same love and acceptance she'd always given Courtney and him. Even before their father had dumped them here after their mother ran off with her personal trainer. "That's why I developed Fair Face's new line of animal products."

Ignoring the gray dog brushing against his leg, Caleb held up his hands to stop her. "Fair Face doesn't manufacture animal products."

Grams's grin didn't falter. "Not yet, but you will. I've tested the formulas on my consultant and myself. We've used them on my dogs."

"I didn't know you hired a consultant."

"Her name is Becca. You'll love her."

Caleb doubted that. Most consultants were only looking for a big payday. He'd have to check this Becca's qualifications. "You realize Fair Face is a skin care company. Human skin."

"Skin or fur. Two legs or four. Change…expansion is important if a company wants to remain relevant."

"Not in this case." He needed to be careful not to hurt Grams's feelings. "Our resources are tied up with the launch of the organic baby care line. This isn't the time to expose ourselves to more risk."

Lines tightened around her mouth. "Your grandfather built Fair Face by taking risks. Sometimes you have to put yourself out on a limb."

"Limbs break. I have one thousand one hundred thirty-three employees who count on me to make sure they receive paychecks."

"What I'm asking you to do is not risky. The formulas are

ready to go into production. Put together a pilot sales program and we're all set."

"It's not that simple, Grams. Fair Face is a multinational company. We have extra product testing and research to ensure ourselves against liability issues." The words came out slowly, full of intent and purpose and zero emotion. His grandmother was the smartest woman he knew, used to getting her way. If he wasn't careful, he would find himself not only manufacturing her products, but also taking one of her damn dogs home. Likely the one-eyed mutt with soft fur. "I won't expose Fair Face to the additional expense of trying to break into an unknown market."

Grams sighed, a long drawn out sigh he hadn't heard since Courtney lost her passport in Prague when she was supposed to be in Milan.

"Sometimes I wish you had a little more of your father in you instead of being so buttoned-down and by-the-book."

The aggravation in her voice matched the tension cording in Caleb's neck. The tightness seeped to his shoulders, spilled down his spine. "This isn't personal. I can't afford to make a mistake, and you should be enjoying your retirement, not working in your lab."

"I'm a chemist. That's what I do. You didn't have this problem with the organic baby line." Frustration tinged each of her words, matching the I-wish-you'd-drop-it look in her eyes. "I see what's going on. You don't like the dog care products."

"I never said that."

"But it's the truth." She studied him as if she were trying to prove a hypothesis. "You've got that look. The one you got when you said it didn't matter if your father came home for Christmas."

"I never needed him here. I had you and Gramps." Caleb would try a new tactic. He scooted his chair closer. "Remember Gramps's marketing tagline."

"The fairest face of all..."

"His words still define the company today. Fifty years later."

Caleb leaned toward her, as if his nearness would soften the blow. "I'm sorry to say it, but dog products, no matter how natural or organic or aromatherapeutic, have no place at Fair Face."

"It's still my company." She enunciated each word with a firm voice punctuated by her ramrod posture.

Disappointing his grandmother was something his father did, not Caleb. He felt like a jerk. One with a silk noose around his neck choking him.

"I know that, but it's not just my decision." A plane flew overhead. A dog barked. The silence at the table deepened. He prepared himself to say what he'd come here to say. "I met with the department heads before coming over here. Showed them your prototypes. Ran the numbers. Calculated margins."

"And…"

"Everyone has high expectations for your baby skin care line," he said. "But they agree—moving into animal products will affect Fair Face's reputation, not enhance our brand and lead to loss of revenue, anywhere from 2.3 to 5.7 percent."

Caleb expected to see a reaction, hear a retort. But Grams remained silent, her face still, nuzzling the dog against her neck. "Everyone thinks this?"

He nodded once.

Disbelief flickered across her face. She'd looked the same way when she learned his grandfather had been diagnosed with Alzheimer's. But then something sparked. A spark of resignation. No, a spark of resolve.

"Well, that settles it. I trust you know what's best for Fair Face." She sounded doting and grandmotherly, not disappointed and hurt. "Becca and I will figure out another way."

"Another way for what?"

Grams's eyes darkened to a steely blue. "To manufacture the products. You and those suits at Fair Face are wrong. There's a market for my dog skin care line. A big one."

The sun's rays warmed Becca Taylor's cheeks. The sweet scent of roses floated on the air. She walked across the manicured lawn in Gertie's backyard with two dogs—Maurice, a Norwegian elkhound, and Snowy, a bichon frise.

The two show dogs sniffed the ground, looking for any dropped treats or a place to do their business.

She tucked her cellphone into her shorts pocket. "Don't get sidetracked, boys. Gertie is waiting for us on the patio."

Becca had no idea what her boss wanted. She didn't care.

Gertie had rescued Becca the same way she'd rescued the foster dogs living at the estate. This was only a temporary place, but being here gave them hope of finding a forever home.

Maurice's ears perked.

"Do you hear Gertie?"

The two dogs ran in the direction of the patio.

Becca quickened her pace. She rounded a corner.

Gertie and a man sat at the teak table underneath the shade of the umbrella. Five dogs vied for attention, paws pounding on the pavement. Gertie waved.

The man next to her turned around.

Whoa. Hello, Mr. Gorgeous.

Tingles skittered from Becca's stomach to her fingertips.

None of the dogs growled or barked at the guy. Points in his favor. Dogs were the best judges of character, much better than hers.

She walked onto the patio.

The man stood.

Another wave of tingles made the rounds.

Most guys she knew didn't stand. Didn't open doors. Didn't leave the toilet seat down. This man had been raised right.

He was handsome with classical features—high cheekbones, straight nose, strong jawline. The kind of handsome women showed off to girlfriends.

The man stepped away from the table, angling his body toward her. His navy pinstriped suit was tailored, accentuating wide shoulders and tapering nicely at the hips. He moved with the grace of an athlete, making her wonder if he had sexy abdominal muscles underneath.

Very nice packaging.

Well, except for his hair.

His short, cookie-cutter, corporate hairstyle could be seen walking out of every high rise in downtown Boise. With such a gorgeous face, the man's light brown hair should be longer, a little mussed, sexy and carefree, instead of something so... businesslike.

Not that his hair mattered to Becca. Or anything about him.

His top-of-the-line suit shouted one thing—Best in Show.

She might be a dog handler, but she didn't handle his type.

They didn't belong in the same ring. He was a champion with an endless pedigree. She was a mutt without a collar.

She'd tried playing with the top dogs, the wealthy dogs, once before and landed in the doghouse, aka jail.

Never again.

But looking never hurt anybody.

Gertie looked up from the dogs at her feet. "Becca. There's someone I want you to meet."

He was tall, over six feet. The top of her head came to the tip of his nose.

Becca took two steps closer. "Hello."

His green eyes reminded her of jade, a bit cool for her taste, but hey, no one was perfect. His eyelashes more than made up for whatever reserve she saw reflected in his gaze. If she had thick, dark lashes like his she would never need to buy mascara again.

She wiped her hand on her shorts then extended her arm. "I'm Becca Taylor."

His grip was strong, his skin warm.

A burst of heat shot up her arm and pulsed through her veins.

"Caleb Fairchild." His rich voice reminded her of melted dark chocolate, rich and smooth and tasty.

Wait a minute. Fairchild. That meant he was...

"My grandson," Gertie said.

The man who could make Becca's dream of working as a full-time dog handler come true. If the dog products sold as well as Gertie expected, Becca would have the means to travel the dog show circuit without needing to work extra part-time jobs to cover living expenses.

Caleb Fairchild. She couldn't believe he was here. That had to mean good news about the dog products.

Uh-oh. Ogling him was the last thing she should be doing. He was the CEO of Fair Face and wealthy. Wealthy, as in she could win the lottery twice and not come close to his net worth.

"Nice to meet you." Becca realized she was still holding his hand. She released it. "I've heard lots about you."

Caleb's gaze slid over her as if he'd reviewed the evidence, passed judgment and sentenced her to the not-worth-his-time crowd. "I haven't heard about you until today."

His formal demeanor made Jane Austen's Mr. Darcy seem downright provincial. No doubt Mr. Fairchild thought he was too good for her.

Maybe he was.

But she wouldn't let it bother her.

Her career was not only at stake, but also in his hands.

"Tell me about yourself," he said.

His stiff tone irritated her like a flea infestation in the middle of winter. But she couldn't let her annoyance show.

She met his gaze straight on, making sure she didn't blink or show any signs of weakness. "I'm a dog person."

"I thought you were a consultant."

A what? Becca struggled for something to say, struggled and came up empty. Still she had to try. "I…I—"

"Becca is a dog consultant," Gertie said. "She's a true dog whisperer. Her veterinary knowledge has been invaluable with product development. I don't know what I'd do without her."

If Becca wasn't already indebted to Gertie Fairchild, she was now.

Gertie shot a pointed look at Caleb. "Perhaps if you dropped by more often you'd know what's going on."

Caleb directed a smile at his grandmother that redefined the word *charming*.

Not that Becca was about to be charmed. The dogs might like him, but she was…reserving judgment.

"I see you every Sunday for brunch at the club." Caleb's affection for his grandmother wrapped around Becca like a thick, warm comforter, weighing the scales in his favor. "But you never talk about yourself."

Gertie shrugged, but hurt flashed in her eyes so fast Becca doubted if Caleb noticed. "Oh, it just seems like we end up talking about you and Courtney."

"Well, I'm here now," he said.

Gertie placed her hand over her heart and closed her eyes. "To dash all my hopes and dreams."

Becca's gaze bounced between the two. "What do you mean?"

Caleb touched Gertie's arm. "My grandmother is being melodramatic."

Opening her eyes, Gertie pursed her lips. "I'm entitled to be a drama queen. You don't want our pet products."

No. No. No. If that was true, it would ruin…everything. Gertie wouldn't go forward with the dog products without her company backing them. Becca forced herself to breathe. "I don't understand."

Gertie shook her head. "My grandson, the CEO, and his closed-minded cronies at *my* company believe our dog skin care line will devalue their brand."

"That's stupid and shortsighted," Becca said.

Caleb eyed her as if she were the bounty, a half-eaten mouse or bird, left on the porch by an outdoor cat. "That's quite an opinion for a…consultant."

"Not for a dog consultant." The words came out more harshly than Becca intended, but if she couldn't change his mind she would be back to living in a singlewide behind Otto. Otto, her parents' longtime trailer park manager, wore stiletto heels with his camouflage, and skinned squirrels for fun. "Do you know how much money is spent annually on pets?"

"Billions."

"Over fifty billion dollars. Food and vet costs are the largest portion, but analysts project over four billion dollars are spent on pet services. That includes grooming. Gertie's products are amazing. Better than anything on the market."

Gertie nodded. "If only my dear husband were still around. He'd jump on this opportunity."

"Gramps would agree with me." Caleb frowned, not a sad one, more of a do-we-have-to-go-through-this-again frown. "Fair Face is not being shortsighted. We have a strategic plan."

Becca forced herself not to slump. "So change your plan."

"Where'd you get your MBA?" he asked.

Try AA degree. "I didn't study business. I'm a certified veterinary technician, but my most valuable education came from The School of Hard Knocks."

Aka the Idaho Women's Correctional Center.

"As I explained to my grandmother, the decision about manufacturing the dog skin care line is out of my hands."

Caleb's polite tone surprised Becca, but provided no comfort. Not after she'd poured her heart and soul into the dog products. "If the decision was all yours?"

His hard, cold gaze locked on hers. "I still wouldn't manufacture them."

The words slammed into Becca like a fist to her jaw. She took a step back. But she couldn't retreat. "How could you do this to your grandmother?"

Caleb opened his mouth to speak.

Gertie placed her hand on his shoulder. "I'll help Becca understand."

He muttered a thank-you.

"This decision is in the best interest of Fair Face." Gertie sounded surprisingly calm. "It's okay."

But it wasn't.

Becca had thought that things would be different this time.

That she could be a part of something, something big and successful and special. That maybe, just maybe, dreams could come true.

She should have known better.

Things never worked out for girls—women—like Becca.

And never would.

CHAPTER TWO

A FEW MINUTES LATER, Becca stood where the grass met the patio, her heart in her throat and her back to Gertie and Caleb. Dogs panted with eagerness, waiting for the ball to be thrown again.

And again. And again.

Playing fetch kept Becca's shoulders from sagging. She would much rather curl up in the kennel with the dogs than be here. Dogs gave her so much. Loyalty, companionship and most importantly love. Dogs loved unconditionally. They cared, no matter what. They accepted her for who she was without any explanations.

Unlike…people.

"Come sit with us," Gertie said.

Us.

A sheen of sweat covered Becca's skin from the warm temperature, but she shivered.

Caleb had multi-millions. Gertie had hundreds of millions. Becca had $8,428.

She didn't want much—a roof over her head, a dog to call her own and the chance to prove herself as a professional handler. Not a lot to ask.

But those dreams had imploded thanks to Caleb Fairchild.

Becca didn't want to spend another minute with the man.

She glanced back at her boss.

"Please, Becca." Gertie's words were drawn out with an

undertone of a plea. Gertie might be more upset about Fair Face not wanting to take on her new products than she acted.

Becca whipped around. Forced a smile. Took a step onto the patio. "Sure, I'll sit for a few minutes."

Caleb was still standing, a tall, dream-crushing force she did not want to reckon with ever again.

Walking to the table, she didn't acknowledge his presence. He didn't deserve a second look or an "excuse me" as she passed.

Gertie had to be reeling, the same as Becca, after what he'd said.

I still wouldn't manufacture them.

Becca's blood boiled. But she couldn't lose it.

She touched Gertie's thin shoulder, not knowing how else to comfort her employer, her friend. The luxurious feel of silk beneath Becca's palm would soon be a thing of the past. But it wasn't the trappings of wealth she would miss. It was this amazing woman, the one who had almost made Becca believe anything was possible. *Almost...*

"I'm so sorry." A lump burned in her throat. Her eyes stung. She blinked. "You've worked so hard and wasted so much time for nothing."

Gertie waved her hand as if her arm were an enchanted wand that could make everything better. Diamonds sparkled beneath the sun. Prisms of lights danced. If only magic did exist....

"None of this has been a waste, dear." Gertie smiled up at Becca. Not the trying-hard-to-smile-and-not-cry of someone disappointed and reeling, but a smile full of light and hope. "The products are top-notch. You said so yourself. Nothing has changed, in spite of what Caleb thinks."

He gave a barely perceptible shake of his head.

Obviously he didn't agree with his grandmother. But Gertie didn't seem deterred.

That didn't make sense to Becca. Caleb was the CEO and

had final say. She sat next to Gertie. "But if Fair Face doesn't want the products…"

"You and I are starting our own company." Gertie spoke with a singsong voice. "We'll manufacture the products without Fair Face."

Our own company. It wasn't over.

Becca's breath hitched. Her vision blurred. She touched her fingers to her lips.

The dream wasn't dead. She could make this work. She wasn't sure how…

Gertie had always spoken as if working with Fair Face on the products was a done deal, but if going into business was their only option that would have to do. "O-kay."

"Your consultant doesn't sound very confident," Caleb said to Gertie. "Face it, you're a chemist, not a businesswoman." He looked at Becca. "Maybe you can talk some sense into my grandmother about this crazy idea of hers."

Becca clenched her hands. She might not know anything about business, but she didn't like Caleb's condescending attitude. The guy had some nerve discounting his grandmother.

Forget jade. The color of his eyes reminded her of cucumbers or fava beans. Not only cool, but uninspiring.

Change and *taking a risk* weren't part of his vocabulary. But they were hers. "Makes perfect sense to me. I'm in."

"Wonderful." Gertie clapped her hands together. "We'll need an advisor. Caleb?"

A horrified look distorted his face, as if he'd been asked to face the Zombie Apocalypse alone and empty-handed. He took a step back and bumped into a lounge chair. "Not me. I don't have time."

His words—dare Becca say excuse?—didn't surprise her. The guy kept glancing at his watch. She'd bet five bucks he had his life scheduled down to the minute with alarms on his smartphone set to ring, buzz or whistle reminders.

"You wouldn't leave us on our own to figure things out." Gertie fluttered her eyelashes as if she were some helpless female—about as helpless as a charging rhino. "You'll have to make the time."

His chin jutted forward. Walking across burning coals on his hands looked more appealing than helping them. "Sorry, Grams. I can't."

Good. Becca didn't want his help any more than he wanted to give it. "We'll find someone else to advise us."

Gertie grinned, the kind of grin that scientists got when they made a discovery and were about to shout "Eureka!" "Or…"

"Or what?" Becca said at the same time as Caleb.

"We can see if another company is interested in partnering with us." Gertie listed what Becca assumed to be Fair Face's main competitors.

Caleb's lips tightened. His face reddened. His nostrils flared. *Well played, Gertie.*

Becca bit back a smile. Not a scientific breakthrough, but a way to break Caleb. Gertie was not only intelligent, but also knew how to get her way. That was how Becca had ended up living at the estate. She wondered if Caleb knew he didn't stand a chance against his grandmother.

"You wouldn't," he said.

"They are my formulas. Developed with my money in my lab here at my house," Gertie said. "I can do whatever I want with them."

True. But Gertie owned the privately held Fair Face.

Becca didn't need an MBA from a hallowed ivy-covered institute to know Gertie's actions might have repercussions.

Caleb rested his hands on the back of the chair. One by one, his fingers tightened around the wood until his knuckles turned white.

Say no.

Becca didn't want him to advise them. She and Gertie needed help starting a new business. But Becca would rather not see Caleb again. She couldn't deny a physical attraction to him. Strange. She preferred going out with a rough-around-the-edges and not-so-full-of-themselves type of guy. Working-class guys like her.

Being attracted to a man who had money and power was stupid and dangerous. Men like that could ruin her plans. Her life. One had.

Of course, Caleb hadn't shown the slightest interest in her. He wouldn't. He would never lower his standards. Except maybe for one night.

No, thanks.

Becca wanted nothing to do with Caleb Fairchild.

Caleb was trapped, by the patio furniture and by his grandmother. This was not the way he'd expected the meeting to go. He was outnumbered and had no reinforcements. Time to rein in his grams before all hell broke loose.

He gave her a look, the look that said he knew exactly what she was doing. Too bad she was more interested in the tail-wagging, paw-prancing dogs at her feet. No matter, he knew how to handle Grams. Her so-called consultant was another matter.

Becca seemed pleased by his predicament. She sat with her shoulders squared and her lips pursed, as if she were looking for a fight. Not exactly the type of behavior he would have expected from a consultant, even a dog one.

He would bet Becca was the one who talked Grams into making the dog products. Nothing else would explain why his grandmother had strayed from developing products that had made her and Fair Face a fortune.

It had to be Becca behind all this nonsense.

The woman was likely a con artist looking to turn this consulting gig into a big pay off. She could be stealing when Grams wasn't paying attention. Maybe a heist of artwork and jewelry and silver was in the works. His wealthy family had always been a target of people wanting to take advantage of them. People like Cassandra. Grams could be in real danger.

Sure, Becca looked more like a college student than a scammer. Especially wearing a "No outfit is complete without dog hair" T-shirt and jean shorts that showed off long, smooth, thoroughbred legs.

She had great legs. He'd give her that.

But looks could be deceiving. He'd fallen for Cassandra and her glamorous façade.

Not that Becca was glamorous.

With her short, pixie-cut brown hair and no makeup she was pretty in a girl-next-door kind of way. If he'd ever had a next-door neighbor whose house wasn't separated by acres of land, high fences and security cameras.

But Becca wasn't all rainbows and apple pie.

Her blue eyes, tired and hardened and wary, contradicted her youthful appearance. She wasn't innocent or naïve. Definitely not one of the princess types he'd known at school or the social climbers he knew around town. There was an edge to her he couldn't quite define, and that…intrigued him.

Worried him, too.

He didn't want anyone taking advantage of Grams.

Speaking of which, he faced his grandmother. "It's not going to work."

Grams glanced up from the dogs. The five animals worshipped at her feet as if she were a demigod or a large slice of bacon dressed in pink. "What's not going to work, dear?"

A smile tugged on the corners of Becca's mouth, as if she were amused by the situation.

Caleb pressed his lips together. He didn't like her.

Any consultant with an ounce of integrity would have taken his side on this. But what did he expect from a woman who wore sports sandals with neon-orange-and-green toenail polish to work? He bet she was covered with tattoos and piercings beneath her clothing.

Sexy images of her filled his mind.

Focus.

He rocked back on his heels. "If you partner with one of Fair Face's competitors, the media will turn this into a firestorm. Imagine how the employees will react. You're the creative influence behind our products. How will you reconcile what you do for one company with the other?"

"Animal products for them. Human products for Fair Face." A sheepish grin formed on Grams's lips. "It was only a thought."

A dog tried to get his attention, first rubbing against Caleb's leg then staring up at him. Seemed as if everyone was giving him the soulful-puppy-look today. "A ploy."

Grams tsked. "I can't believe you think I'd resort to such a tactic."

Yeah, right. Caleb remembered looking at what colleges to attend and Grams's reaction. Naval Academy, too dangerous. Harvard, too far. Cal Berkeley, too hippy. She'd steered him right where she'd wanted him—Stanford, her alma mater. "I'm sure you'd resort to worse to get your way."

That earned him a grin from Becca.

Glad someone found this entertaining. Though she had a nice smile, one that made him think of springtime and fresh flowers. An odd thought given he had little time to enjoy the outdoors these days. Maybe it was because they were outside.

"I shouldn't have to resort to anything," Grams said. "You promised your grandfather you'd take care of us."

Something Caleb would never forget.

That promise was directing the course of his life. For better or worse given his grandmother, his sister, Fair Face and the employees were now his responsibility. He grimaced. "I'm taking care of you the best way I know how."

Grams rubbed a gray dog named Blue, but she didn't say a word.

He knew this trick, using silence to make him give in, the way his grandfather had capitulated in the past. But Caleb couldn't surrender. "Grams—"

"Gertie, didn't you mention the other day how busy Fair Face keeps your grandson?" Becca interrupted. "It might be better to find someone else to help us, since Caleb is so busy."

Whoa. Becca wanted to be his ally?

That sent Caleb's hinky-meter shooting into the red zone. No one was that nice to a total stranger. She must want him out of the way so she could run her scam in peace.

"Good idea," he said, playing along. Maybe he could catch Becca in a lie or trip her up somehow. "I'm not sure I'd have a few minutes to spare until the baby product line launches, if then. You know how it is."

"Yes, I do." Grams tapped her fingers against her chin. "But I like keeping things in the family."

So much for taking her formulas to a competitor. "You wouldn't want me to ignore the company, would you?"

His grandmother's gaze narrowed as if zooming in on a target—him. "Who's trying to guilt who now?"

He raised his hands in surrender. "Fair enough."

"Maybe Caleb knows someone who can help us," Becca said.

He would rather his grandmother drop this whole thing, but once Grams saw what starting her own business entailed, she would decide retirement was a better alternative. He would get someone he trusted to advise them, someone to keep an eye on Becca, someone to steer his grandmother properly. Caleb would still be in control, by proxy. "I'm happy to give you a few names. I know one person who would be a good fit."

"I suppose it's worth a try," Gertie said.

"Definitely worth a try." Enthusiasm filled Becca's voice. "We can do this."

We? Us? Caleb straightened. Becca acted more like a partner. He needed to talk to his grandmother about what sort of contract she had with her "consultant." Something about Becca bothered him. She had to be up to no good. "I'll text you the names and numbers, Grams."

"Send Becca the list. As you said, I'm a chemist not a businesswoman."

"Will do." Caleb glanced at his watch, bent and kissed his grandmother's cheek. "Now, if you ladies will excuse me, I need to get back to the office."

Grams grabbed hold of his hand. Her thin fingers dug into his skin. "You can't leave. You haven't had any cake."

The carrot cake. Caleb had forgotten, but he couldn't forget the pile of work waiting for him on his desk. He checked his watch again.

"Gertie baked the carrot cake herself. You need to try a piece." Becca's voice sounded lighthearted, but her pointed look contained a clear warning. Caleb had better stay if he knew what was good for him.

Interesting. The consultant was being protective of his grandmother. Usually that was *his* job. Becca's concern could be genuine or a ruse—most likely the latter—but she was correct about one thing. Eating a slice of cake wouldn't take *that* long. No reason to keep disappointing Grams. He could also use the opportunity to ask his grandmother for more information about her dog consultant.

Caleb placed his arm around his grandmother. "I'd love a piece of your cake and a glass of iced tea."

Dogs raced around Becca, jumping and barking and chasing balls. She stood in the center of the lawn while Gertie went into the house to have Mrs. Harrison prepare the refreshments.

Playing with the dogs was more fun than sitting with Caleb on the patio. Becca saw no reason to make idle chitchat with a man eager to eat his cake and get out of there. At least, she couldn't think of one.

She much preferred four-footed, fur-covered company to dismissive CEOs. Dogs were her best friends, even when they were a little naughty.

"You're a mess, Blue." Becca picked strands of grass and twigs from the Kerry blue terrier's gray hair. "Let's clean you up before Gertie returns."

Dogs—no matter a purebred like Blue or a mutt like Dozer—loved to get dirty. Gertie didn't mind, but Becca tried to keep the dogs looking half decent even when playing.

Blue licked her hand.

Bending over, she kissed his head. "Such a good boy."

"You like dogs."

Becca jumped. She didn't have to turn around to know Caleb was right behind her, but she glanced over her shoulder anyway. "I love dogs. They're my life."

His cool gaze examined her as if she were a stock he was deciding to buy or sell, making her feel exposed. Naked.

Her nose itched. Her lungs didn't want to fill with air.

He stepped forward to stand next to her. "Your life as a dog consultant?"

"Gertie came up with that title," Becca said. "But I am a dog handler, groomer and certified vet tech."

"A jill of all trades."

That was one way to look at it. Desperate to make a living working with animals and to become a full-time professional dog handler was another. "When it comes to animals, particularly dogs."

Snowy and Maurice chased each other, barking. Dozer played tug-of-war with Hunter, a thirteen-inch beagle, growling. Blue sat at Becca's feet, waiting. "I need to put the dogs in the kennel."

Confusion clouded Caleb's gaze. He might as well have spoken the question on his mind aloud.

"Yes, Gertie has a kennel."

"How did you know what I was thinking?"

"Your face." Becca almost laughed. "I'm guessing you don't play a lot of poker. Unless you prefer losing money."

Caleb looked amused, not angry. That surprised her.

"Hey," he said. "I used to be quite good."

"If the other players were blind."

"Ha-ha."

"Well, you don't have much of a poker face."

At least not with his grandmother. Or with Becca.

He puffed out his chest. "We're not playing cards. But you're looking at a real card shark."

She liked his willingness to poke fun at himself. "I believe you."

"No, you don't."

Heat rushed up her neck. "Okay, I don't."

"Honest."

"I try to be." He wasn't talking about poker any longer. She picked up one of the balls. "It's important to play fair."

Caleb's eyebrow twitched. "Do you have a good poker face?"

"You realized I didn't believe you, so probably not."

"No aces up your sleeve?"

"Not my style."

"What is your style?"

"Strategy over deceit." Becca couldn't tell if he believed her, but she hoped he did. Because he was Gertie's grandson, she rationalized. "That's why I'd never sit at a poker table with you. You're too easy to read. It would be like stealing a bone from a puppy."

"A puppy, huh?"

"A manly pup. Not girly."

He grinned wryly. "Wouldn't want to be girly dog."

His gaze held hers. Becca stared mesmerized.

Something passed between them. A look. A connection.

Her pulse quickened.

He looked away.

What was going on? She didn't date guys like him. Even if she did, he was too much of a Boy Scout. And it was clear he didn't like her. "I have to go."

"I want to see the kennel."

"Uh, sure." But she felt uncertain, unsettled being near him. She pointed to the left. "It's down by the guest cottage."

Caleb fell into step next to Becca, shortening his stride to match hers. "How did you meet my grandmother?"

She called the five dogs. They followed. "At The Rose City Classic."

He gave her a blank stare.

Funny he didn't know what that was, given Gertie's interest in dog showing. "It's in Portland. One of the biggest dog shows on the West Coast. Your grandmother hired me to take Snowy into the breed ring. Ended up with a Group third. A very good day."

Blue darted off, as if he were looking for something—a toy, a ball, maybe a squirrel.

Becca whistled for him.

He trotted back with a sad expression in his brown eyes.

Caleb rubbed his chin. "I have no idea what you just said."

"Dog show speak," Becca said. "Snowy won third place in the Group ring. In his case, the Non-Sporting group."

"Third place is good?"

"Gertie was pleased with the result. She offered me a job taking care of her dogs, including the fosters and rescues, here at the estate."

"And the dog skin care line?"

"She sprang that on me after I arrived."

A look of surprise filled his eyes, but disappeared quickly. "Sounds like you're a big help to her."

"I try to be," Becca said. "Your grandmother's wonderful."

"She is." He looked at her. "I'd hate to see anyone take advantage of her kindness."

Not anyone. Becca.

The accusation in his voice made her feel like a death row inmate. Each muscle tightened in preparation for a fight. The balls of her sandals pressed harder against the grass. She fought the urge to mount a defense. If this were a test, she didn't want to fail. "I'd hate that to happen, too."

The silence stretched between them.

His assessing gaze never wavered from hers.

Disconcerted, she fiddled with a thread from the hem of her shorts.

Caleb put his hand out to Dozer, who walked next to them. Funny, considering he'd ignored the dogs before.

Dozer sniffed Caleb's fingers then nudged his hand.

With a tender smile, he patted the dog's head.

Becca's heart bumped. Nothing was more attractive than a man being sweet to animals. A good thing Caleb's physical appearance was pretty easy to overlook given his personality and suspicions.

"You helped me with my grandmother," he said. "Trying to get me out of the way?"

At least he was direct. She wet her lips, not liking the way he raised her hackles and temperature at the same time. "It's obvious you don't want to work with us."

"I don't have time," he clarified.

"There's never enough time."

Dozer ran off, chasing a butterfly.

"It's a valuable commodity," Caleb said.

"Easy to waste when you don't spend it in the right ways."

"Experience talking?"

"Mostly an observation."

Maurice, the Norwegian elkhound, approached Caleb. The dog could never get enough attention and would go up to anyone with a free hand to pet him.

He bent over.

And then Becca remembered. "Wait!"

Caleb touched the dog. He jerked back. A cereal-bowl-sized glob of dark and light hair clung to his hand. "What the…"

Maurice brushed against Caleb's pant leg, covering the dark fabric in hair also.

Oh, no. She bit the inside of her cheek.

"This overweight husky is shedding all his fur." The frown on Caleb's face matched the frustration in his voice. "Enough to stuff a pillow."

"Maurice is a Norwegian elkhound. He's blowing his coat." The guilty expression on the dog's face reminded her of the time he'd stolen food out of the garbage can. She motioned him over and patted his head. This wasn't the dog's fault. Unlike Caleb, she was used to the shedding, a small price to pay for his love. "They do that a couple times a year. It's a mess to clean up."

"Now you tell me."

His tone bristled, as if she were the one to blame. Becca was about to tell him if he spent any time here with his grandmother he would know about Maurice, but decided against it. If she lightened the mood, Caleb might stop acting so…upset. "Look at the bright side."

His mouth slanted. "There's a bright side?"

"You could be wearing black instead of navy."

He didn't say anything, then a smile cracked open on his face, taking her breath away. "I guess I am lucky. Though it's only dog hair, not the end of the world."

If he kept grinning it might be the end of hers.

Caleb brushed the hair away, but ended up spreading it up his sleeve and onto the front of his suit.

"Be careful." She remembered he had to return to the office. "Or you'll make it…"

"Worse." He glanced down. Half laughed. "Too late."

It was her turn to smile. "I have a lint roller. I can clean up your suit in a jiffy."

Amusement filled his eyes. "I thought you liked dog hair."

"Huh?"

"Your T-shirt."

She read the saying. "Oh, yes. Dog hair is an occupational hazard."

"Yet you keep a lint brush."

"You never know when it'll come in handy."

"Do you make a habit of cleaning men's clothing?"

His tone sounded playful, almost flirty. That made no sense. Caleb wouldn't flirt with her. She rubbed her lips together. "Not, um, usually."

Something—interest or maybe it was mischief—flared in his eyes. "I'm honored."

Nerves overwhelmed her. A guy like Caleb was nothing but trouble. He could be trying to cause trouble for her now.

She took a deep breath. "Do you have other clothes with you? Getting the dog hair off your pants will be easier if you aren't wearing them."

"Easier, but not impossible."

Becca pictured herself kneeling and rolling the lint brush over his pants. Her temperature shot up ten degrees. She crossed her arms over her chest. "You can use the roller brush yourself."

He grinned wryly. "My gym bag is in the car."

An image of him in a pair of shorts and a T-shirt stretched across his muscular chest and arms rooted itself in her mind.

Wait a minute. Did he say gym bag? That meant he had time to work out, but no time to spend with Gertie.

Becca's blood pressure rose, but she knew better than to allow it to spiral out of control. Judging him wasn't right. People did that with her and usually got it wrong. Maybe his priorities had gotten mixed up. She'd give him the benefit of the doubt. For now.

"Go change," she said. "I'll put the dogs in the kennel and grab the lint brush out of guest cottage."

"Using the guest cottage as your office?"

"I live there."

His mouth dropped open. He closed it. "You live here at the estate?"

"Yes."

"Why?"

The one word dripped with so much snobbery Becca felt as if someone had dumped a bucket of ice-cold water on her head.

He waited for her to answer.

A hundred and two different answers raced through her mind. She settled on one. "Because Gertie thought it would be for the best."

"Best for you."

"Yes." But there was more to it than that. "Best for Gertie, too."

Confusion filled his gaze. "My grandmother doesn't lack anything."

He sounded so certain, not the least bit defensive. A good sign, but still…

Becca shouldn't have brought this up, but her affection for Gertie meant Becca couldn't back down now. She wanted Caleb to stop blowing off his grandmother. "Gertie thought living here would make it easier for me to do my job without having to drive back and forth all the time. But I also think she wants me here because she's lonely."

"My grandmother lonely?"

The disbelief in his words irritated Becca. She'd realized this as soon as she got to know Gertie, yet her own grandson couldn't see it. "Yes."

"That's impossible," he said without hesitation. "Gertie Fairchild has more friends than anyone I know. She's a social butterfly who turns down invitations—otherwise she'd never be home. She has the means to go out whenever she wants. She has an entire staff to take care of the house and the grounds. No way is she lonely."

What Caleb said might have been true once, but no longer. "Gertie does have a staff, but we're employees. She has lunch twice a week with friends. But she hasn't attended any parties since I moved in. She prefers to spend time in her lab."

"The lab is keeping her from her friends."

"I believe your grandmother would rather spend time with her family, not friends."

"You believe?" He grimaced. "My sister and I—"

"See her every Sunday for brunch at the club, I know. But since I arrived neither you nor your sister have stopped by. Not until you today."

"As I said—"

"You've been busy," Becca finished for him.

Caleb shot a sideways glance at the house. "All Grams has to do is call. I'll do whatever she asks."

"Gertie asked for your help with the dog care products."

"That's…"

"Different?"

A vein at his neck throbbed. "You've got a cush job living here at the estate. I'm sure my grandmother's paying you a bundle to take care of a few dogs and prance them around the ring. What's it to you anyway?"

He sounded defensive. She would, too. Realizing you'd screwed up was never easy. Boy, did she know that. "Gertie's helped me a lot. I want her to be happy."

"Trust me, she's happy. But you have some nerve sponging off my grandmother, helping her with her wild dog-product scheme and then telling me how I should act with my family."

Not defensive. Overconfident. Cocky. Clueless.

Caleb Fairchild was no different than the other people who saw her as dirt to be wiped off the bottom of their expensive designer shoes.

At least she'd tried. For Gertie's sake.

Becca reached out her hand. "Give me your jacket."

"You're going to help me after trying to make me feel like a jerk?" he asked.

Mission accomplished. If he felt like a jerk he had only himself to blame. "I said I'd help. I only told you the truth."

He didn't look as if he believed her. They were even. She didn't trust him.

"As you see it," he said.

She met his gaze straight on. "I could say the same about your truth."

They stood there locked in a stare down.

Stalemate.

"At least we know where we stand," he said.

Becca wasn't so certain, but she knew one thing. Being with Caleb was like riding a gravity-defying roller coaster. He left her feeling breathless, scared to death, and never wanting to get on again. She didn't like it. Him.

She held up his jacket. "And just so you know, I'm not doing this for you. I'm doing it for Gertie."

CHAPTER THREE

BY THE TIME Caleb changed into a pair of shorts and a T-shirt and then returned to the patio, the table had been transformed with china, crystal glasses and a glass-blown vase filled with yellow and pink roses from the garden. Very feminine. Very Grams. "You've gone all out."

"I enjoy having company." Beaming, Grams patted the seat next to her. "Sit and eat."

Caleb sat next to her. He stared across the table at Becca.

What was she doing here?

He wanted to speak to Grams alone, to talk about Becca and his concerns about the so-called dog consultant and if she was exploiting his grandmother's generosity.

Sneaky scam artist or sweet dog lover? Becca seemed to be a contradiction, one that confused him.

On their way to the kennel, he'd sensed a connection. Something he hadn't felt in over a year. Maybe two. Not since… Cassandra. But he knew better than to trust those kinds of emotions with a total stranger.

Becca wasn't his usual type—Caleb casually dated high-powered professional women—but he'd found himself flirting and having fun with her until she'd had to ruin the moment with her ridiculous grandmother-is-lonely spiel.

Becca was wrong. He couldn't wait to prove how wrong.

He sliced through his cake with his fork. The silver tines pinged against the porcelain plate.

As if he wanted or needed anything from Becca Taylor other than her lint roller.

"You must be hungry," Grams said.

Nodding, he took a bite.

Becca drank from her glass of ice water.

"Do the dogs usually stay in the kennel all day?" he asked.

A rivulet of condensation rolled down her glass. She placed it on the corner of the yellow floral placemat. "No, they are out most of the time, but if they were here they'd be going crazy over the cake."

"Dogs eat cake?" he asked.

Becca refilled her water from a glass pitcher with lemons floating on the top.

A guilty expression crossed Grams's face. "I never give them a lot. Never any chocolate. But when they stare up at me as if they're starving, it's too hard not to give them a taste."

"Those dogs know exactly how to get what they want." Laughter filled Becca's eyes. "They're spoiled rotten."

"Nothing wrong with being spoiled and pampered," Grams agreed.

"Not at all." Becca sounded wistful. "I'd love to be one of your dogs."

Her words surprised Caleb. She didn't seem like the primping and pampering type. But what did he really know about her? He sipped his iced tea.

She picked up her fork and sliced off a bite of cake. Her lips parted.

Fair Face made a lipstick that plumped lips, making them fuller and, according to the marketing department, more desirable. Becca's lips were perfect the way they were.

She raised the fork.

Like a moth to a blowtorch, Caleb watched her, unable to look away. He placed his glass on the table.

She brought the fork closer to her mouth until her lips closed around the end.

The sweat at the back on his neck had caused the collar on his T-shirt to shrink two sizes in the past ten seconds.

She pulled out the empty fork. A dab of enticing frosting was stuck on the corner of her mouth.

A very lickable position.

What the hell was he thinking? Caleb wasn't into licking. At least not his grandmother's employee, one who claimed to know more about Grams's than he did.

The woman was dangerous. Caleb forced himself to look away.

If making him feel worse had been Becca's goal, she'd succeeded. Not only worse, but also aggravated. Annoyed. Attracted.

No, not attracted. Distracted. By the frosting.

His gaze strayed back to the creamy dab on Becca's face.

Yes, that was it. The icing. He placed his fork on the plate. Not the lick…

"Please don't tell me you're finished?" Grams asked, sounding distressed he hadn't eaten the whole slice.

The last thing Caleb wanted was more cake. He needed to figure out what was going on with Becca, then get out of here. "Letting the food settle before I eat more."

He sneaked a peek at Becca.

The tip of her pink tongue darted out, licking her top lip to remove the bit of frosting before disappearing back into her mouth.

Caleb stuck two fingers inside his collar and tugged. Hard. The afternoon heat was making him sweat. Maybe he should head to the gym instead of back to work. Doing today's workout at the gym might clear his head and help him focus on the right things.

He wiped his mouth with a yellow napkin. Becca should have used hers instead of her tongue to remove the icing.

Maybe Becca was trying to be provocative and flirty. Maybe Becca saw dollar signs when she looked at him as Cassandra had. Maybe Becca didn't want him to object to her involvement with Gertie. His grandmother had to be the mark here, not him.

"The cake is delicious. Moist," he said. "The frosting has the right amount of sweetness."

Eyes bright, Grams leaned forward over the table. "I'm so happy you like it. I've been working hard on the recipe."

With a sweet grin that made him think of cotton candy, Becca motioned to her plate. Only half the slice remained. "I think you've perfected it."

Grams chuckled. "Took me enough attempts."

"I've enjoyed each and every slice." Becca patted her trim waistline. "As you can tell."

"Nonsense," Grams said. "You have a lovely figure. Besides, a few slices of cake never hurt anybody. Men like curves, isn't that right, Caleb?"

He choked on the cake in his mouth. Becca's curves were the last thing he should be looking at right now. Not that he hadn't checked them out before. "Mmmm-hmmm."

"See," Grams said lightheartedly.

Warm affection filled Becca's eyes. "I'm sold."

Caleb's gaze darted between the two women. Grams treated Becca more like a friend than an employee. That was typical of his grandmother's interactions with her staff, including the dowdy Mrs. Harrison, a fortysomething widow who preferred to go by her last name.

Still, Grams and Becca's familiarity added to his suspicions given the differences in their social status, personalities and ages. His grandmother always took in strays and treated them well. Becca seemed to be playing along with her role in that scenario, but adding a twist by making sure she was becoming indispensable and irreplaceable.

Something was definitely off here. "Grams is an excellent baker."

"You should have been here on Monday," Becca said. "Gertie knocked it out of the park with her Black Forest cake. Seriously to-die-for."

"Black Forest cake?" he asked.

Grams nodded with a knowing gleam in her eyes. "Your favorite."

That had been only three days ago. Caleb stared at his plate.

Carrot cake was Courtney's favorite. Grams had made his favorite earlier in the week. Puzzle pieces fell into place like colored blocks on a Rubick's Cube. A seven-layer lead weight settled in the pit of Caleb's stomach. "How many cakes do you bake a week?"

"It depends on how long it takes us to eat one," she answered.

The question ricocheted through him, as if he were swinging wildly and hitting only air. "Us?"

"Becca. The estate staff. My lab assistants. Whoever else happens to be working here," Grams explained. "Sometimes Becca takes the leftovers to the vet clinic when she covers shifts there."

Wait a minute. He assumed his grandmother paid Becca well and allowed her to live in the guest cottage rent-free. Why would Becca work at a vet clinic, too? Especially if she was running a con?

"Sounds like a lot of cake." Caleb tried to reconcile what he was learning about Becca as well as Grams's cake. "I didn't realize you enjoyed baking so much."

Grams raised a shoulder, but there was nothing casual or indifferent in the movement. "Can't have one of my grandchildren stop by and not have any cake to eat."

But I also think she wants me here because she's lonely.

Damn. His chest tightened. Becca was right. Grams was lonely. Regret slithered through him.

Thinking about the number of cakes being baked with anticipation and love and a big dose of hope made it hard to breathe. He figured Grams would be out and about doing whatever women of her age did to pass the time. Lunches, museums, fundraisers. He'd never thought she would go to so much trouble or imagined she would be sitting at home and waiting for her grandchildren to stop by.

His promise and his efforts blew up like a fifty-megaton bomb.

So much for taking care of Grams. He'd failed. He hadn't taken care of her. He'd let her down.

Just like his...dad.

Guilt churned in Caleb's gut. He opened his mouth to speak, but wasn't sure what to say. "I'm sorry" wasn't enough. He pressed his lips together.

"Did you have something you wanted to say?" Grams asked.

Caleb looked up. His grandmother was speaking to Becca.

Of course *that* woman would have something to say, a smug remark or a smart-aleck comment to expose his failure aloud. Anything so she could rub a ten-pound bag of salt into the gaping hole over his heart.

"No," Becca said, but that didn't soothe him, because she had an I-told-you-so smile plastered on her face. She looked pleased, almost giddy that she'd been proven correct.

How deeply had she ingrained herself in Grams's life? He was concerned how well Becca could read his family. He needed to find his grandmother a new consultant, one with a better education, wardrobe and manners. One he trusted.

Becca's silly, sheep-eating grin made the Cheshire cat look as if he were frowning. She raised a forkful of cake to her mouth. Each movement seemed exaggerated, almost slow motion as if she knew he was waiting for her to make the next move and she wanted to make him suffer.

Good luck with that.

Caleb couldn't feel any worse than he was feeling. He had to do something to make this up to Grams.

"You can have another slice after you finish yours," Grams said.

"One is enough for today," he said. "But let me know when you bake another Black Forest cake, and I'll stop by."

A dazzling smile on his grandmother's face, the kind that

could power a city for a day, reaffirmed how lonely she must be in spite of her money and friends. That loneliness made her vulnerable to people who wanted to take advantage of her, people like Becca.

"I'll do that," Grams said.

He ground the toe of his running shoe against the tile.

In spite of his thinking he'd been a doting grandson, his phone calls, text messages and brunch on Sunday hadn't been enough. Grams wanted to spend face-to-face time with her grandchildren, to chat with them and to feed them.

Caleb's overbooked calendar flashed in his mind. His arm and shoulder muscles bunched, as if he'd done one too many Burpees at the gym.

He was so screwed.

No, that wasn't right.

This was his grandmother, not some stranger.

He'd made a promise, one he intended to honor if it killed him. And it might do that unless Caleb could figure something out. A way to spend more time with Grams. Make more time for her. Find time…

Becca's fork scraped against the plate.

Food.

That gave him an idea.

He had to eat. So did Grams.

Mealtimes would allow him to eat and appease his grand-mother's need to see her grandson at the same time. The question was how often. Brunch was a standing date. Dinner once a week would be a good start.

"Let's have dinner next week on Wednesday. Invite Court-ney to come," he suggested. "I'm sure your cook can whip up something tasty for us. You can make dessert."

Grams shimmied her narrow shoulders, as if she were a teenager bursting with excitement, not an elderly woman.

Maybe once a week wouldn't be enough. His chest tightened.

"That sounds wonderful," Grams said. "Do you think Courtney can make it?"

The anticipation in Grams's voice made one thing certain. His sister would be at the dinner if he had to buy her a pretty, expensive bauble or a new pair of designer shoes. Grams was worth it. "Yes. She'll be here."

Grams looked as if she might float away like a helium balloon. "Excellent, because I can't wait for Courtney to meet Becca."

Caleb rolled his shoulders, trying to loosen the knots. He didn't want Becca at dinner. The woman had overstayed her welcome as far as he was concerned. This meal was for his family, not employees.

He flashed her a practiced smile, so practiced people never saw through it. But the way Becca studied him made Caleb wonder if she was the exception to the rule. He tilted his head. "Join us for a glass of wine on Wednesday."

Becca brushed her knuckles across her lips. "I don't want to intrude on your evening."

"You aren't intruding," Grams said before Caleb could reply. "You're having dinner with us."

"No," he said at the same time as Becca.

His gaze locked on hers for an uncomfortable second before he looked away. Only ice remained in his glass, but he picked it up and sipped.

The woman was…unpredictable. One more thing not to like about her. He was more of a "load the dice ahead of time so he knew what he was going to roll" kind of guy. He didn't like surprises. He'd bet Becca thrived upon them.

Grams's lip curled. "Caleb."

Becca studied her cake as if a magic treasure were hidden inside. "It's okay, Gertie."

No, it wasn't. Caleb deserved his grandmother's sharp tone. "What I meant is Courtney is a lot to take in if you're not used to being around her. I have no doubt they'll name a Category 5 hurricane after her one of these days."

"Your sister can be…challenging at times," Grams said.

Understatement of the year. Courtney was the definition

of drama princess. The rest of the earth's population was here to make his sister look good or help her out. Nothing he tried stopped her from being so selfish. Not even making her work at Fair Face in order to gain access to her trust fund. "We don't want Courtney to overwhelm Becca and make her want to hightail it out of here."

On second thought getting Becca out of the picture was exactly what he wanted to happen. No way would Grams start a business venture on her own. Caleb might have to rethink this.

"Becca won't be overwhelmed. She's made of stronger stuff than that," Gertie said.

"Thanks, but you need this time alone with your grandchildren." Becca's eyelids blinked rapidly, like the shutter on a sport photographer's camera. "I can't make it anyway. I'm covering a shift for a vet tech at the twenty-four hour animal hospital on Wednesday."

"That's too bad," he said.

She toyed with her napkin, her fingers speeding up as if someone had pressed the accelerator. A good thing the napkin was cloth or it would be shredded to bits.

"It is," Becca said. "But I'm sure you'll have a wonderful time together."

Her saccharine sweet voice sounded relieved not to be a part of the dinner. Maybe she had seen through him. That would be a first. "You'll be missed."

As much as a case of poison oak.

A dismayed expression crossed Grams's face, washing over her like a rogue wave. Her shoulders hunched. "You're working that night, Becca?"

The tremble in her voice sent Caleb's pulse accelerating like a rocket's booster engine. Unease spiraled inside him. He reached for his grandmother's hand, covering hers with his. Her skin felt surprisingly warm. Her pulse wasn't racing. Good signs, he hoped. "Grams? You okay?"

She stared at her hands. "I forgot about Becca working on

Wednesday. I do have an assistant who reminds me of things, but…"

Grams shook her head slowly, as if she were moving through syrup not air.

Caleb understood her worry. His grandfather had suffered from Alzheimer's, a horrible disease for the patient as well as the family. Being forgotten by the man who'd held their lives together for so long hadn't been easy. But even at the worst of times, Grams had dealt with the stress of the disease with raw strength and never-ending grace and by making jokes. He'd never seen his grandmother act like this. Not even when she'd been stuck in bed with an upper respiratory infection over a year ago. "No worries. You've had a lot on your mind."

"That's right," Becca agreed.

Caleb wondered if she knew something about Grams's health, but hadn't told anyone. Except Becca looked genuinely concerned.

Grams gave his hand a feeble squeeze. "I should be able to remember a detail like Becca's work schedule."

"I never told you about next week's schedule." Becca's voice was soft and nurturing and oh-so-appealing. "I received the call this morning about what shifts I'll be covering. You haven't forgotten anything."

"I haven't?" Grams asked.

Hearing the unfamiliar uncertainty in her voice worried Caleb.

"Nope," Becca confirmed.

Whether his grandmother had forgotten or not, she seemed so much older and fragile. Time to call her doctor. He patted her hand.

"I'm going to stick around this afternoon." This would cause havoc with his schedule, but he needed to be here for Grams. He could use the time to figure out what was going on with Becca. "I can finish up my work here, then we'll have dinner."

Grams straightened. All signs of weakness disappeared like a wilted flower that had found new life. Her smile took twenty years from her face. Her eyes twinkled. She pulled her hand from beneath his and rubbed her palms together. "That will be perfectly splendid."

Huh? Her transformation stunned him.

"Maura, the new cook, is making lasagna tonight. She's using my recipe for the sauce," Grams said to him. "Becca loves my sauce, don't you?"

Amusement gleamed in Becca's eyes. "I do."

Caleb didn't know what she found so funny. His grandmother's health was nothing to laugh about. "Sounds great, but let's phone your doctor first."

"Nothing is wrong with me." Grams waved off his concern, as if he'd asked if she wanted a slice of lemon in her iced tea. "I had a complete physical two months ago. Dr. Latham said I'm healthy, with a memory an elephant would envy."

That didn't explain what had happened with her only moments ago. "A call won't take long."

Grams's lips formed a perfect O. She leaned toward him. "You're worried about me."

No sense denying the obvious. He nodded.

She touched the side of his face, her touch soft and loving. "You have always been the sweetest boy."

He blew out a frustrated puff of air. "I haven't been a boy for a while."

"Very true, but I remember when you ran around the house naked." She looked at Becca while heat rose in his cheeks. "He never wanted to wear clothes unless it was a superhero costume or camouflage."

Forget the doctor. Might as well call the coroner. For him. Cause of death—embarrassment. "I was what? Three?"

"Three, four and five. It seems like yesterday," Grams said with a touch of nostalgia. She stood. "Please don't worry about me. I'm fine."

Caleb wasn't sure about that. He rose.

She motioned him to sit. "Eat the rest of your cake. I'm going to tell Mrs. Harrison you're staying for dinner."

"I'll go with you," he said.

Becca gave him the thumbs-down sign.

Caleb would have to be blind to misinterpret that signal. He sat. "Or I can finish my cake."

"Do that. Then use the study to work." The words were barely out of Grams's mouth before she bounced her way toward the house.

The French doors slammed shut.

Caleb leaned over the table toward Becca. He might not like her. He sure as hell didn't trust her, but she was the only one he could ask. "What is going on with my grandmother?"

Becca understood Caleb's concern. She'd been worried, too, until she realized Gertie was faking her memory loss. Becca glanced at the house, biting back a smile. "I imagine your grandmother's in a mad rush to get to the pantry for the ingredients for a Black Forest cake."

Caleb's eyes darkened to an emerald-green. Make that the color of steamed broccoli. His mouth pinched at the corners. "What?"

"You know how you talked about your grandmother using ploys to get her way?"

His gaze narrowed. "Yes."

"Gertie played both of us by pretending to be a forgetful granny."

"She wouldn't."

"She did." It was all Becca could do not to bust out in a belly laugh. "You'd better work on your poker face or prepare for more of her antics, since it worked so well."

"Huh?"

"You not only stayed for cake, but you're having dinner here."

He rubbed the back of his neck. "Grams played me like a well-tuned Stradivarius, didn't she?"

"Perhaps not that well-tuned."

"Touché."

"Your grandmother is the smartest woman I know."

"You seem pretty sharp yourself."

Warmth emanated from Becca's stomach. She hoped the heat didn't spread all the way to her face. No one except Gertie had ever called Becca sharp. "Thanks, but what she was doing wasn't hard to figure out."

"What tipped you off?" he asked.

He leaned back in his chair, looking more relaxed and comfortable. Different. More approachable. The workout clothes looked mouthwateringly good on him.

"Becca?"

Oops. She'd been staring. Her cheeks warmed. A pale pink, she hoped. "I hadn't told Gertie about my work schedule. But when she looked at your hand on hers and didn't look away, I knew something was up."

"I thought it was strange, but Grams knows how to push my buttons when she wants. She had me worried about her health."

"Desperation can drive a person to do things they normally wouldn't."

He tossed Becca one of those you've-got-to-be-kidding looks. "My grandmother is not desperate."

"I'd be desperate if someone I loved kept blowing me off."

"You don't have to keep rubbing it in. I'm going to spend more time with her."

"Glad to hear it." Becca had expected Caleb to be angry, not repentant. This softer side of him surprised her, given his obvious suspicions about her. Appealed to her, too. "You have no idea how lucky you are. Gertie is amazing. Don't take her for granted."

"You really seem to care about Grams."

Becca nodded. "I wish she was my grandmother."

"Do you have family close by?" he asked.

"Southern Idaho. I don't see them much." Becca didn't like the conversation turning toward her. She stood. "I have to go."

Caleb scooted back in his chair. "Where are you going?"

"To get your suit."

"Before you go." He stood. "One question."

"What?"

"Are Grams's dog products that good?"

"Will you believe what I say?"

"I asked your opinion."

He hadn't answered her question. Maybe he had a better poker face than she thought. "The products are so excellent, they'll sell themselves."

"You sound certain. Confident."

"I am," she said. "The line is going to make a fortune, but it's better that Fair Face isn't manufacturing the products."

His jaw tensed. "I thought that's what you and Grams wanted."

"It was, but not now."

"Trying to get rid of me?"

"Sort of."

His eyes darkened. "Why is that?"

"If Fair Face doesn't believe in the products, they won't be willing to put all their resources behind them," she said. "Fair Face will do enough, just enough, to appease Gertie. The line might not fail, but it won't succeed as well as it could with the right backing and support."

"For a dog consultant, you know a lot about business."

Becca hated that his words meant as much as they did. They shouldn't. "Not really. It's common sense."

"Not having Fair Face involved means more money for you."

She hadn't thought about that. "More money would be great."

"I'm sure it would be."

As if Caleb could understand what money would mean to her. He'd never gone hungry because there wasn't enough money for groceries. He'd never worn thrift-shop clothes and duct-taped shoes. He'd never left prison with nothing except a backpack and an appointment with a probation officer.

"Thinking about how you're going to spend all that money?" he asked.

"Thinking about our next step," she said. "I'll give you my number. Text me the names and numbers of possible advisors."

"No need."

Her heart dropped. "What do you mean?"

"I know the perfect person to help you and Grams."

She fisted her hands in anticipation. "Who?"

"Me."

No. No. No. Every nerve ending shrieked. "You said you didn't have time."

"That was before you made me realize I've been neglecting my grandmother and should spend more time her."

Oh, no. Becca had brought this upon herself. "You should be doing something fun with Gertie, not working with her."

"You said she liked to work."

"She does. But…" Becca swallowed. "You don't want to ignore Fair Face."

"I'll work it out. This way I'll be able to help you, too." He sounded so confident, as if nothing could stop him. "I can answer any questions you have, make sure things stay on track, maybe provide angel funding. That should make you happy."

The lopsided smile on Caleb's face told Becca he expected her to be anything but happy about this. Goal achieved, because she was very unhappy at the moment. "I—"

"Trust me."

She would never trust a man with so much money and power. She chewed the inside of her cheek. "I hate to put you out like this. It really isn't necessary."

"No worries. Honest." The charming smile spreading across his face made her breath hitch. "Besides, I'm not doing this for you. I'm doing it for my grandmother."

CHAPTER FOUR

THE NEXT AFTERNOON, Caleb left his office and rode in a limousine to his grandmother's estate. He hoped the element of surprise would work in his favor today. Unlike yesterday when he'd been caught off-guard by most everything.

Spending time with Grams and being her advisor were the perfect ruses for Caleb dropping by unannounced. He could keep on eye on Becca until he figured out what she was up to.

The estate's housekeeper, Mrs. Harrison, answered the door. She told him that Grams was in the lab, which he expected, and Becca was in the study, which he hadn't.

Every nerve ending went on alert.

She shouldn't be allowed to have free rein on the estate. She shouldn't be allowed to sit in the same study where his grandfather put together Fair Face. She shouldn't be here at all.

He stood in the doorway of the study, watching Becca.

With a laptop at her left, she hunched over the desk, pencil in hand, scribbling notes on paper. She wore a green T-shirt. He assumed she had on shorts, but he saw only crossed long legs and a bare foot swinging beneath the desk.

"Working hard?" Though he imagined her brainstorming ways to con Grams out of money rather than actual work.

Becca's gaze jerked up. Her eyes widened. She set her pencil on the desk. "Caleb. I didn't know you were stopping by."

"I thought I'd see if you have any questions about the business plan we talked about last night."

"That's what I'm working on."

Convenient. Unless she was lying. He took a step toward her. "Let me see what you've done."

She frowned. "I only started this morning."

"I'm your advisor," he said in an even voice. No reason to make her aware of his suspicions. "It's my job to keep you headed in the right direction."

And make sure she didn't hurt what mattered most to him.

Becca eyed him warily. "I didn't realize CEOs micromanage their employees."

"You don't work for me." If Becca did, he would have fired her yesterday when she gave away her true intention.

Trying to get rid of me?

Sort of.

Not sort of. He had no doubt she'd wanted him gone so she could scam Grams out of as much money as possible. That was why he'd agreed to advise them, why he'd participated in a conference call on the way over here, why he'd be checking in with them daily.

To protect Grams. To protect Fair Face.

"But I'm advising you." For now. He'd hired a private investigator to do a background check, but until the man reported back Caleb was sticking close to her, even if it messed up his schedule. "I take that role seriously."

She straightened the papers and handed the stack to him. "Here."

He ran his thumb over the edges. Too many to count quickly. "A lot of pages for starting this morning."

Her mouth tightened. "I didn't plagiarize, if that's what you're suggesting."

Her defensive behavior suggested she knew Caleb was onto her. No reason to be all that subtle about his suspicions. Maybe she'd get scared and take off on her own. That would make things simpler, especially with Grams.

Tension, thick and unsettling, hung in the air.

Underneath the desk, her foot swung like a pendulum

gone crazy. Back and forth, speeding up each time the blur of fluorescent-painted toenails came toward him.

"I wasn't suggesting anything." Caleb didn't trust Becca. But he couldn't deny she…intrigued him. He held the papers in the air. "Only making an observation."

"I found a business plan template online," she said to his surprise. "The website explains what to write where and gives you text boxes to fill in. You download the plan into word processing software."

"Handy."

"Yes."

Caleb read through her rough draft, making mental notes as he went. He set the plan on the desk.

"So?" she asked, her voice full of curiosity.

"Not bad." He waited for a reaction, but didn't get one. She either didn't care or had tight control of her emotions. He would go with apathy. "Hold off on working on the executive summary until the business plan is complete. That way you'll have a better idea of who and what the company is all about."

She rested her elbows on the desk and leaned forward. Her V-neck T-shirt gaped, giving him an enticing peek of ivory skin, beige satin and cleavage.

He enjoyed the view for a moment, felt his temperature rise and then looked away. This wasn't the time to be distracted by a nice, round pair of breasts.

"What else?" she asked.

Becca sounded interested, not apathetic, as if she wanted to know what was wrong and how to fix it. That was unexpected.

Caleb picked up the business plan and scanned the pages again. He'd read through enough business plans over the years with his personal venture capital/angel fund to offer some quick fixes. "This is a good start, but you need specific goals and a more concrete direction. The product descriptions are excellent, but you're missing pricing information or market comparisons. You'll need hard facts, start-up costs, projected balance sheets. 'The products will sell themselves' isn't a sales and marketing strategy."

Her shoulders slumped. "There's so much more to this than I realized."

"That's what I was trying to tell you and my grandmother yesterday." The more discouraged they got, especially Becca, the better. "There are easier ways to make money than starting your own business."

She stared at her hands. "Making money has never come easy for me or people I know."

"My grandfather told me hard work always pays off."

"I've heard your grandfather was a wonderful man, but sometimes hard work doesn't put groceries in the cupboard." Without a glance Caleb's way, she made notes on another piece of paper. "Anything else I should add?"

"Make these fixes first, then I'll review it again." He handed back her pages. "Writing something like this is an iterative process."

"That sucks, since Gertie wants the plan finished tonight."

Grams could be impatient. When she'd presented the baby products, she'd wanted them on the market in less than three months. It had taken almost a year. "I'm surprised she didn't want it done yesterday."

"Two dogs needed baths last night. Otherwise, she would have told me to get it done. In a nice way, of course."

Grams could be firm, but "in a nice way" described her perfectly. "When did you move in?"

"February."

Four months ago. Had it been that long since he'd been to the estate? He couldn't remember. "You've had plenty of time to figure out how my grandmother operates."

"She's the best boss. Ever."

So adamant. Loyal. The woman deserved an Oscar nomination for her acting abilities. "Grams likes getting her way."

Becca stared down her nose at him. "Most people do."

"You?"

"If it ever happened, I'd probably like getting my way."

If. Probably. Her words raised more questions.

"But I never get my way," she added. "Let me tell you. It sucks."

Caleb had never met a woman like Becca Taylor. She might be a scammer, but the way she spoke her mind was…entertaining. She added color and expectation into predictable life. He would miss that when she was gone. But he would survive.

The next day, Becca finished her morning run with Maurice. She walked to the kennel with the dog at her side.

Sweat covered her face and dripped from her hair. Her legs trembled from the exertion. "Let's get you put away so I can see what Gertie needs."

"My grandmother wants you up at the house."

The sound of Caleb's voice sent goosebumps prickling Becca's skin. A strange sensation, given how sticky and hot she felt at the moment.

But strange and Caleb seemed to go together. Three visits in three days. For someone claiming to be busy, he had a lot of time to check up on—make that "advise"—her. Though today was Saturday, and based on his casual attire, a pair of cargo shorts and a T-shirt, he wasn't going into the office today.

"You run," he said.

"The dogs run." She opened the kennel door. The blast of cool air refreshed her, kept her temper in check. "I hold the leashes and get dragged along."

"You're not a runner."

"Do I look like a runner?" She glanced back at him. "Don't answer that."

Caleb smiled, but whether his smile was genuine or not remained to be seen. He followed her into the kennel, the door closing behind him. "Why do you run if you don't like it?"

She not only didn't like running, she didn't like Caleb being underfoot. His wide shoulders and height made the spacious kennel feel cramped and stuffy.

"Some of the dogs prefer it to walking." Becca opened the door to Maurice's space complete with pillow bed and a doggy door that led to his own grassy dog run. She unhooked his leash and let him loose inside. The dog went straight for his stainless steel water bowl. "So we run."

"You really are a dog person."

"Muscle tone is important. Dog judges don't like to see flabby or fat dogs in the ring."

"You run the little ones, too?"

"I walk them." She checked each of the dog bowls to make sure they had enough water to get them through the next couple of hours. "How briskly depends on their legs."

"When do you walk them?" he asked.

"I already did." She wished he'd go bother someone else. Maybe he was trying turn on the charm and play nice. But he looked good today. He exuded confidence, and a part of her wanted to reach out and grab some for herself. That was bad. Becca didn't want to notice anything about Caleb Fairchild. She was thinking about him too much as it were. Maybe she was lonely. An animal control officer she'd met at the animal hospital had mentioned meeting for coffee. Going on a date with him might take her mind off Caleb. "They'll get another walk later if it's not too hot."

"Sounds like they are lucky dogs."

"Anyone who is fortunate to have Gertie on their side is a lucky dog."

"Including you?"

"I'm the luckiest." She motioned to the door. "I need to see what Gertie wants."

"I'll go with you."

Figures. "I'm sure you want to spend as much time with your grandmother as possible."

"That's right."

Liar. Becca bit her tongue to keep from saying the word aloud. Caleb spent twice as much time with her than Gertie.

Okay, his insights on the business plan had been useful.

Becca would give him that much credit. But the way Caleb watched her, as if trying to catch her doing something wrong made her so self-conscious she was having trouble sleeping. Something she hadn't had since leaving prison. She didn't like it. Didn't like him.

Maybe if she kept working hard and proved herself writing the business plan, Caleb would continue visiting his grandmother, but leave Becca alone. She hoped so because whenever he came close physical awareness shot through her like an electric shock.

She found Gertie, dressed in a lab coat and black pants, sitting on a bar stool at the kitchen's island. Mrs. Harrison washed vegetables. A young woman named Maura, who helped cook and clean, stood at the stove, stirring whatever was inside a saucepan.

"You wanted to see me," Becca said.

"Yes." Gertie clapped her hands together. "I have some news. A sort of good news/bad news kind of thing."

Becca had never known Gertie to have any bad news until today. "Start with the bad so we end on a high note."

"I can't go with you to the dog show in Oregon next weekend," Gertie announced.

Becca's chest tightened. She took a step forward. "Is anything wrong?"

"Oh, no, dear. I'm fine, but I found out an old friend is being thrown a surprise party. It's not something I can miss."

That wasn't really bad news. Not compared to some of the bad news she'd dealt with in the past. She would miss Gertie's company, but her employer needed to get out of the lab more. "Go have fun. I'm used to doing shows on my own."

"You won't be alone." Gertie bounced from jeweled slipper to jeweled slipper and back again. "That's my good news. Caleb is going with you so he can see the products in action."

No. No. No.

Becca staggered back until she bumped into something solid and around six feet tall.

Caleb.

She jumped forward. "Sorry."

"No worries."

Maybe not for him, but this wasn't good news at all. A weekend with Caleb watching her every move, waiting and hoping she screwed up. Not to mention the strange way he made her insides quiver. She couldn't let this happen. "Have you ever been to a dog show before?"

"No, but I need to know how the products work in order to help you."

Caleb would hate wasting time at a dog show. She had work to do, but he would be standing or sitting around, bored out of his mind. She wouldn't have time to entertain him or be subjected to another of his inquisitions.

There had to be a way to convince him not to go.

On Monday, the clip of Caleb's Italian leather wingtips against the estate's hardwood floor echoed the beat of his heart. Working with Becca on the business plan, he'd learned two things about her: she was from a small town outside Twin Falls, Idaho, and her father's first name was Rob. Information his private investigator had used to perform a background check.

The jig was up. Caleb had known his instincts were right about her.

His hand tightened around the manila folder containing irrefutable proof Becca Taylor was trying to scam his grandmother. He strode into the estate's solarium with one goal in mind—get Becca away from his grandmother. "Hello, Grams."

"Caleb." She lounged on a chaise holding a glass of pink lemonade complete with a pink paper umbrella. "Thanks for letting yourself in. I was standing most of the day, and my feet hurt."

He kissed her cheek. "You shouldn't spend so much time in the lab."

"It's what I do."

Not for long. The crazy dog care line would soon be nothing but a footnote in Grams's life, a distant memory along with Becca. He crinkled the edge of the folder. "Where's your consultant?"

"At the animal hospital." Grams placed her drink on a mosaic end table she'd purchased in Turkey. "You're stuck with me."

"I came to visit you."

Grams placed her hand on her chest. "I'm touched. What did you want to talk about?

He sat in a damask covered chair next the chaise. "Becca."

Grams's eyes softened with affection. "Becca has been spending so much time writing and revising the business plan. You'll be impressed."

Caleb doubted that, but he reminded himself to be conscious of his grandmother's feelings. "I learned disturbing news today. Becca Taylor isn't who you think she is."

"I know exactly who Becca is." Grams sounded one hundred percent confident. "She's a sweet, hardworking woman and my friend."

One who takes, takes, takes before hightailing it out of there.

"Your friend Becca, aka Rebecca Taylor, is a convicted criminal. She spent three years at the Idaho Women's Correctional Center." Caleb expected to see a reaction, but didn't. Maybe Grams was trying to take it all in. "We're not talking shoplifting, Grams. Theft, trespassing and vandalism."

Grams tapped her finger against her cheek. "How did you find out?"

"A private investigator." He raised the folder in the air, careful to keep his excitement out of his voice. "I know you consider Becca a friend and she's been helping you, but she's taking advantage of you. Fire her. Get her out of the guesthouse. Out of your life. Before she hurts you and robs you blind."

"Just because a person makes a mistake in the past doesn't mean they'll repeat it in the future."

"She is a crook." He didn't understand why his grandmother

was being so understanding. She should be upset, furious. Maybe she was in shock. "I'll bet Becca learned more ways to break the law while she was in jail."

Grams picked up her pink lemonade and stared into the glass. "Becca told me all about her time in prison."

"You knew about this?"

"She told me everything before she accepted my job offer."

Outrage choked him. "Yet you hired her anyway? Let her move in?"

"She made a youthful mistake."

He scoffed. "That mistake landed her in jail."

"She paid the price for her actions. Learned her lesson."

"We're not talking about an overdue library book." He stared at his grandmother in disbelief. "You can't have a criminal working for you. It's not safe."

"Becca would never hurt me."

"She is a convicted—"

"I respect her honesty and integrity," Grams interrupted. "I'm not going to hold the past against her. Neither should you."

"Don't make me out to be the bad guy here. I didn't rob anybody," he countered. "I'm trying to look out for you, Grams. That's what Gramps wanted me to do. You have a big heart. People have taken advantage of you in the past."

"People need the opportunity to make a fresh start."

Caleb's jaw tensed. "You gave my father plenty of fresh starts. He blew every single one."

"Becca is nothing like him."

"That's true," Caleb agreed. "My father was never in jail."

"Your father had his own issues," Grams said. "But even if he'd gone to jail, it wouldn't have changed the way I felt about him. People deserve another chance."

Everyone meaning Becca. And…his father.

A weight pressed down on Caleb's chest, squeezing the air out of his lungs and the blood out of his heart. "How many fresh starts did you give my father?"

"If your father were alive today, I'd be giving him another

chance the way I'm doing with Becca. That's what you do when you love someone."

"Rebecca Taylor is a complete stranger."

"To you. Not to me. I care what happens to her," Grams said. "And I'm much more interested in the woman she is today than the girl she was at eighteen."

Caleb pressed his lips together. This wasn't how he'd imagined the conversation going. "You don't know if she's told you the truth. Read the report, then you can decide—"

"I've made my decision about Becca. Nothing is going to change my mind, but you should talk to her about this and appease your concerns."

"You're that sure about her."

"Yes," Grams said. "I want you to be sure about Becca, too. Talk to her about your concerns. Let her explain what happened."

That would be a complete waste of time.

Nothing Becca had to say would change his mind.

Absolutely nothing.

Grams's eyes implored him. "Please, Caleb. Speak with Becca. For me."

Screw Caleb Fairchild for delving into her business.

Becca balled her hands. The tenth floor of Fair Face's corporate headquarters was the last place she wanted to be tonight.

"Mr. Fairchild will see you now," a middle-aged uniformed security guard said. "Follow me."

Becca walked down an empty hallway. The fifth draft of the business plan inside her gray-and-black messenger bag bumped against her hip.

She adjusted the bag's strap. She wasn't even sure why she'd brought the plan along. Maybe to show Caleb she'd been working, not plotting a crime against his grandmother.

As if he would believe her.

She glanced at the guard. "It's quiet."

"Most folks have gone home," he said.

The carpet muted their footsteps, unlike the correction facility where sound echoed. Instead of passing walled cells with solid metal doors and slits for windows, she passed offices with mahogany wood doors and brass nameplates. No one whispered her name or called her something nasty. No one shot dagger-filled stares or tried to beat her up when the guards weren't looking.

But the memories hit her hard. The sounds. The smells. The bone-chilling cold she could never seem to shake even during the long, hot summers.

Becca crossed her arms over her chest.

She wanted to forget about all that. Not relive the worst three years of her life to appease Caleb Fairchild's curiosity. But she would talk to him…for Gertie's sake.

At the end of the hallway, the guard pointed to an office with its door open. A light was on inside. "That's Mr. Fairchild's office."

She wondered if Mr. Fairchild had asked the guard to stick around outside his office while they spoke. After all, she was a hardened criminal. She forced a tight smile. "Thanks."

She entered the office.

Big. She hadn't expected the office to be this large, complete with a round table surrounded by six chairs, a couch and coffee table, a large desk, chairs, bookcases along her right side and floor to ceiling windows on the two far corner walls.

Then again, Caleb Fairchild was the CEO.

He sat at his desk, a portrait in concentration as he stared at his computer monitor.

Caleb looked every bit the handsome business executive—if you liked that type. Even though it was past quitting time, every strand of his hair was in place, his tie knotted tightly around his neck and his sleeves unrolled. The only thing missing was his suit jacket.

He looked clean cut, respectable and proper. But as with Whit who'd gotten her in so much trouble, Becca knew looks could be deceiving. Caleb was a shark waiting to attack and take her out. Exactly the sort she tried to avoid. But tonight she was venturing into his water without a harpoon or any way to defend herself except her word against his suspicions.

It wasn't going to be pretty.

Though he still hadn't noticed her, so maybe she had a chance of surviving. She cleared her throat.

Caleb's cool, assessing gaze met hers.

A chill shivered down her spine.

He stood. "Good evening, Becca."

She saw nothing good about it. He had some nerve hiring a P.I. As if she would have lied about her past to his grandmother. She'd dealt with enough liars and fakes growing up and while she was in jail to ever want to be one.

Becca bit the inside of her cheek.

"Close the door so we have some privacy," he said.

She hadn't seen another person in the building except the security guard. Guess he would be hanging around out in the hallway. Figured. She closed the door.

"Thanks." He motioned to one of the two black leather chairs in front of the large desk. "Have a seat."

Standing wouldn't give her that much of an advantage over sitting seeing as she was out of her element and on his home turf. She crossed his office, removed her messenger bag then sat, sinking into a chair. She ran her fingertips along the buttery soft leather. This furniture was much nicer than anything in her parents' house. "Gertie said you had questions for me."

His gaze didn't waver from Becca's. "You don't waste any time."

Her temperature increased. No doubt stress from his hawk-like gaze. He saw her as a vulture circling over his grandmother. "You've made it clear you're a busy man."

He walked around the front of the desk and sat on the edge.

Needing something to do with her hands, Becca picked dog hair off her skirt.

She'd spent an hour trying to figure out what to wear, finally deciding on one of her dog-show suits—teal skirt, matching three-quarter-sleeve jacket and a lace-trimmed camisole underneath. She wasn't sure what the proper attire was for explaining one's prison record, but this was better than a pair of Daisy Duke shorts and a camisole.

"Tell me how you ended up in prison," he said matter-of-factly.

Becca took a deep breath. She glanced around the room, not really seeing anything. She took another breath, then met his gaze directly. "I was an idiot."

He drew back with confusion in his eyes. "Excuse me?"

"I did something really stupid." Becca rubbed her face. "I fell for a guy. I thought he liked me, so I trusted him. Big mistake."

One corner of Caleb's mouth rose, but she wouldn't call it a smile. Not a half-one, either. "You're not the first to be led astray by their heart."

He sounded as if he'd been there, done that, got the T-shirt. But being led astray and wearing prison garb for three years were totally different things.

Becca had been so naive to think a rich boy like Whitley would want her—a girl from the trailer park. Yet he'd made her feel so…different. Special. Glamorous. Trying to be cool had enticed her to be reckless. She raised her chin. "I should have known better. Whitley was the brother of a girl I'd gotten to know through dog showing. They were wealthy. I wasn't. But Whit didn't seem to care."

"Whit is the man."

"Boy," she clarified. "I couldn't believe when he asked me out for a smoothie. I wanted him to like me, so I tried to be the type of girl he'd want to date, even if that wasn't who I was. I fell…hard."

So hard she'd found herself thumbing through a bridal magazine at the grocery store and imagining what color dresses the bridesmaids should wear. "I'd recently graduated high school. It was summertime. We went out almost every night and then…"

Memories hit strong and fast. The flashing of red and blue

lights. The accusations. The tears. The handcuffs scraping her wrists. Being read her Miranda rights.

Someone touched her shoulder.

She jumped.

Caleb held up his hands as if surrendering. His eyes were dark. Concerned. "Sorry. You looked miles away for a second."

Not miles, years. She stood, backing away from him. "Just…remembering."

"This is hard for you."

Becca nodded, not trusting her voice. A compassionate person would tell her to stop.

Not Caleb.

He didn't say a word, but remained perched on his desk as if he might attack at any minute. Not so much a shark now—more like a dangerous hawk ready to swoop down on his prey.

On her.

A thrill fissured through her. So not the reaction she should have around him.

Becca shouldn't react to him at all. Or notice all these little details about him.

She hated that she did.

CHAPTER FIVE

BECCA WALKED TO one of the bookcases, the one closest to the office's door and farthest away from Caleb. Oh, he was handsome and could turn on the charm faster than she could blink. Tonight she saw an edge to him she hadn't see before, an edge that appealed to her.

But she knew his type all too well.

Whatever she said tonight would fall on deaf ears. He'd been suspicious of her since the day they met. Nothing was going to change his mind about her.

He'd likely agreed to attend the dog show, not to see the new products in action, but to watch her because of her criminal past.

"I'm not a bad person," she said.

"I never said you were."

But he hadn't said she wasn't, either.

No one cared about the truth. "Guilty" was all that mattered to people. What happened hadn't been forgotten. And wouldn't be. It followed her everywhere.

Or had until she'd met Gertie.

Caleb wouldn't be as understanding. That was why this was so hard for Becca.

She noticed a black-framed photo of him and another man. Both men were attractive. The other guy wasn't as handsome as Caleb, but as fit with a muscular V-shaped physique. A triangle folded American flag with military ribbons sat on the shelf above the picture.

Becca realized she was procrastinating. Might as well get this over with. She looked over at Caleb.

His dark gaze met hers. "Take your time."

"I don't want to drag this out any longer." Telling him what had happened was the only thing that would loosen the tension in her neck. "Whit asked if I wanted to hang out with him and some of his friends. I said yes, thinking things must be getting serious if he wanted to introduce me to his friends."

"A reasonable assumption."

"Reasonable, but wrong," she admitted. "He was interested in me, but not as a girlfriend. I was being set up to be the patsy. The scapegoat. The one they could blame if their plans to break in to the bank president's house to steal cash to buy drugs went south."

"They don't sound like the Honor Society kids."

"Some were. Others were jocks. But they were no better than a gang of hoodlums. They just wore designer clothes and drove nice cars."

"You were part of it."

"No. I had no idea what they were planning." She forced herself not to make a face at him and read the titles of the business books on the shelf instead. A few military strategy type books were mixed in with the marketing and finance titles. "Whit said we were going to hop the fence and go hot-tubbing while the guy was on vacation. I was wearing my bikini underneath my clothing and had a towel crammed in my bag."

But not even those things, including the panties and bra she'd brought to change into, had mattered to the police.

"It wasn't until we were inside the house and not in the backyard that I realized what they were planning. But I thought Whit liked me, so I..."

Becca bit her lip. She couldn't bring herself to say the words.

"You went along," Caleb finished for her.

She nodded. Embarrassed, regretful and ashamed. "I was

trying to fit into Whit's world. I was afraid to speak up, so I just followed his lead."

"I take it things didn't turn out as planned."

"No one knew about the high-tech security system in the house. The police caught us inside, and then..."

Her chest tightened with Whit's betrayal. Becca took a breath and another. It didn't help. "Everyone turned on me. Pointed their fingers at me. Blamed me. They said it had been all my idea. I had picked the lock. Stolen the money."

"But the police should have—"

"The police believed them. Why wouldn't they? My dad had spent time in the county jail for getting into a fight. I was the resident trailer trash. No one was surprised to find me involved in something like this. Not to mention my fingerprints were all over the evidence."

Caleb's eyes widened. "How did that happen?"

She understood the disbelief in his tone. Her parents and lawyer had sounded the same way. "Whit had me wrapped around his little finger. *Open the door, gorgeous. Hold this tool, beautiful. Have you ever seen this much money before? Want to hold it?*"

She hadn't, and she did.

"But the other kids were accessories to the crime," he said. "Whit, too."

"True, but they had high-priced attorneys who managed to get the charges reduced or dropped."

"That doesn't seem fair."

"It wasn't. But life has never been fair to people like me." Caleb's privileged upbringing would affect one's perspective as much as growing up in a trailer park had hers. "Luck wasn't on my side, either. I'd turned eighteen two days before, so was legally considered an adult. My parents couldn't afford a lawyer so I was assigned a public defender. Due to the evidence and witnesses..."

"Whit and his friends cut a deal."

Becca nodded. "My lawyer recommended a plea bargain."

"You took it."

"I wanted to fight the charges, but my parents thought three years in prison was better than the alternative, so I did what my lawyer wanted."

Caleb didn't say anything.

That didn't surprise her. She stared at a photograph of Caleb surrounded by bikini-clad supermodels. There was another picture of the Fairchild family—Caleb, a young woman who must be Courtney, Gertie and her late husband. All four people looked so happy and carefree with bright smiles on their faces.

Becca wondered what it would be like to feel so happy and content. Just once she would like to know.

"You must have been scared," Caleb said.

"Terrified." She still was some days, but he didn't need to know that. "I understand if you don't believe me. But it's what happened."

"A hard lesson to learn."

She walked back to the chair, but remained standing. "I wouldn't wish the three years I spent locked up on anybody. Not even the kids who set me up me that night."

"Regrets?"

"I know people say you shouldn't have regrets, but if I could go back to change that one night I would. Being in jail…it sucked. But I learned my lesson. I'm not going to try to be someone I'm not ever again."

She waited for him to ask the inevitable questions about whether she was part of a gang or if she had a girlfriend or something else he might have seen on television.

"I'm sorry," he said finally.

Her gaze jerked up. "Excuse me."

"I'm sorry you had to go through that."

She didn't say anything. She wasn't sure what to think of his words or the sentiment behind them.

"So what happened after you got out of jail?" he asked.

"I tried to start where I left off. But it wasn't as easy as I thought that it would be."

"Why not?"

"I kept filling out applications and being turned down for job interviews. Even though I'd done my time, people still saw me as a criminal."

He shifted positions on the desk. "What did you do?"

"I'd been planning to go to college to become a vet tech before all this happened, so applied to a few programs and eventually got accepted to one. I used the scholarships I'd won through dog showing and worked every odd job I could find to cover tuition. But after I had my degree, I ran into the same problems as before. I couldn't find a veterinary clinic back home that would hire me."

"Your past."

"My past is very much my present. I fear it always will be. As our conversation tonight proves once again."

He stared at the carpet.

Feeling guilty? Becca hoped so, and she wasn't going to back down. "They say you can't be tried twice for the same crime, but that's only in a court of law. People don't forget, and they hold a grudge. I moved to Boise because I thought I'd have more opportunities here."

"Have you?"

"A few," she said. "I found a job at an animal hospital. A professional dog handler I'd known through 4-H as a kid and as a junior handler in AKC took pity on me and asked if I wanted to be her apprentice. That's how I met Gertie."

"My grandmother doesn't care about your past."

"Gertie is one in a million." Thinking about Gertie made Becca want to smile for the first tine since she'd left the estate earlier. "I wish more people were like her. But they're not."

They were more like Caleb.

That was one reason she preferred the company of dogs to people. Dogs were more loyal, understanding, loving.

"Any other questions?" she asked. "I'm happy to give you the name of my former probation officer. Though he can't guarantee I'm not trying to scam your grandmother."

A blush colored Caleb's cheeks. "She told you."

"She warned me."

"This isn't personal." He sounded defensive. "I'm only trying to protect her."

"As you should," she agreed. "If I weren't your target, I'd say your chivalry is sweet even if it's…misguided. But this isn't the first time it's happened to me. I know it won't be the last."

"You're resigned to that."

"Annoyed by it, too. But what am I going to do?"

Nothing she'd done so far had changed people's opinion of her. But that hadn't stopped her from trying. From working the worst shifts at the animal hospital to busting her butt doing whatever Gertie asked, Becca had wanted to earn people's respect, to be…accepted for who she was now. Not who she'd been before.

"You could move out of Idaho," he said.

"I'm far enough away from my parents as it is."

"Family is important to you."

"It's all I've got."

"Me, too," he said.

A warm look passed between them. Becca found herself getting lost in Caleb's eyes. What was going on? She never expected to have anything in common with Caleb. Well, except for liking chocolate cake and Gertie. But he was more complicated and different from what Becca expected.

"Grams told me you've been working on a revised business plan. Did you bring it with you?" he asked.

"Business plan?" She blinked at the sudden change of topic. "I have it. But I didn't think you were still going to advise us."

"Why not?"

"You only agreed because you had doubts about me."

"That's true."

Her heart fell. Spilling her guts hadn't changed anything. She shouldn't feel as disappointed as she did. "You still have doubts."

"I told my grandmother I would help her," he said. "I'm not going back on my word."

She respected Caleb for being a man of his word, especially when his agreeing had meant so much to Gertie. But he hadn't denied still having doubts about Becca.

That had happened before.

It would happen again.

But she was surprised how much it hurt now.

Caleb was wrong about Becca.

Wrong about her motives. Wrong about her past.

He loosened his tie.

Caleb had misjudged her. Completely.

What she'd said about struggling after getting out of prison jibed with the private investigator's report. She'd admitted her father had spent time in jail, too.

Her education and experience wouldn't give her the knowledge to pull off a big financial scam. Though he couldn't deny the possibility of a theft on a smaller scale.

He glanced up from Becca's business plan.

In her teal suit, standing by one of his bookcases, she looked like a consultant. Professional. Knowledgable. A world apart from the woman he'd met in his grandmother's backyard.

But whether dressed to the nines or in bright orange prison garb, she was the same woman. A woman eager to rebuild her life. A woman he found himself wanting to learn more and more about.

Her story about Whit sounded all too plausible to Caleb. He knew guys like that, his father was like that, his experience with Cassandra had been like that.

Becca was most likely exactly what she seemed to be—a hopeful dog whisperer who was caught up in one of his grandmother's schemes through no fault of her own.

Moving a foot away from him, Becca pulled out a book, read the inside flap, then placed it back on the shelf. She did the same with another.

Con artists, like his Cassandra, were good at sob stories, but Becca seemed too genuine, her behavior too natural and awkward and uncomplicated. She didn't appear to be a threat, but he'd deal with her if that changed.

For now, Caleb would go along with his grandmother's gamble. A part of him admired Becca. That was rare.

But he still had to be careful for all their sakes.

"You're welcome to borrow any of the books," he said.

"Is there one you'd recommend?"

"Strategic Marketing and Branding."

Becca touched each of the book spines with her fingertip, searching for the title. She pulled one out. "Here it is."

"You know the market and the industry, but having a thought out branding strategy can make all the difference," he explained. "The book will be a good introduction to the buzzwords and approaches being used."

She studied the front cover. "Thanks."

"You're welcome."

He thought she would walk back toward his desk. She didn't. Instead she kept looking at the items on the shelves.

"The USS *Essex*." Becca studied one of the small replicas of aircraft carriers. "Gertie has a larger version of this in her collection."

"Gramps was assigned to the USS *Essex* during the Korean War. He fell in love with aircraft carriers. Grams used to give him the models on special occasions."

"What a wonderful gift." Becca bent to take a closer look at the shelf containing the models. Her skirt rose in the back, showing off her firm thighs. "The USS *Vinson*."

His groin tightened. He tried not to stare. "Yes."

"I've seen that one, too." She straightened. "Your grandfather had large replicas at home and small models here at the office?"

"The smaller ones are mine."

She glanced his way. "Yours?"

He nodded, a part of him wishing she could be his tonight.

Whoa. Where had that come from?

He'd been working too hard if his mind was going…there.

Grams hadn't mentioned if Becca had a boyfriend, but Caleb imagined she did. A man who thought nothing of carrying lint rollers, doggy treats and poop bags wherever he went.

Someone totally opposite to Caleb.

He couldn't keep a plant alive, let alone be responsible for a pet. It wouldn't be fair to a dog or cat or fish.

Not that he wanted a girlfriend. He dated when he had time, but kept things…light. It was easier that way, given his schedule.

He secured her pages with a binder clip. "Excellent work on the business plan."

A smile tugged at her lips. He waited for one to explode and light up her face. The right corner lifted another quarter of inch before shooting back into place as if she'd realized she was going five miles per hour over the speed limit and needed to slow down before getting pulled over.

She smiled for Grams, but not him.

That bothered Caleb. He wanted a smile.

Becca bit her lip, gnawing at it like a piece of jerky, a stale piece. "I don't think it's ever going to be ready."

"Iterative process, remember?"

She shrugged.

Ah-ha. A perfectionist. Caleb had a couple on his staff—hard workers—but their never-satisfied, not-good-enough tendencies made end-of-the-quarter more stressful. "What you've done so far is pretty impressive."

Something—pride, maybe?—flashed in her eyes. But the same wariness from before quickly took over. "You think?"

He nodded. "It's obvious you've been working hard revising the drafts."

"That's what Gertie pays me to do."

"You're doing it very well." He would have known that if he'd listened to his grandmother instead of telling her to fire her consultant. He was sure Grams wouldn't let him forget that, either.

Becca straightened, as if he'd finally gotten her attention. Or she liked what he'd said.

"There are a few areas where you'll need to do more research," he added.

"Manufacturing, for sure. And the product containers are giving me a real headache." She was one step ahead of him. "Everything is priced based on quantity. Making that initial order seems to be based on magic."

"A Magic 8 Ball, actually."

"You're…" Her gaze narrowed. "Kidding."

"Had you going for a minute," he teased.

Amusement gleamed in her eyes. "Twenty seconds tops."

"Forty at least."

Her smile burst across her face like the sun at dawn.

He couldn't breathe.

"Thirty," she said playfully. "Not a nanosecond longer."

With her eyes bright and her face glowing, she looked… gorgeous. It was his turn to speak, but Caleb didn't know what to say. All he could do was stare.

She studied him. "Have you ever consulted a Magic 8 Ball?"

"No, but my sister Courtney had one. Swore it worked."

"And you kidded her about that."

"I'm her older brother. Of course I did."

"I'm not surprised," Becca said. "You're not the kind of person who leaves things up to chance, let alone a fortune-telling game."

Interesting observation and dead-on. "Why do you say that?"

She motioned to the books on the shelf. "The business books mixed in with military ones. Strategy. War. That suggests you like to be prepared. Know what you're up against. Have a solid plan and an exit strategy. You take a tactical approach. At least you did with me."

"I may have had some bad intel."

"It happens."

She didn't sound upset. That was a relief. "You're observant."

Becca lifted one shoulder. "I keep my eyes open so I know what's going on."

A lesson learned. No doubt because of what had happened to her when she was younger. Caleb was the same way thanks to Cassandra. Interesting that he and Becca had been used in similar ways. Though hers had been much worse. "It's not good being caught off-guard."

"Nope." She motioned to the other shelf with his memorabilia. "Was the flag your grandfather's?"

"Yes. From his funeral."

She pointed to one of the photographs. "Who's this?"

Caleb crossed the office, picked up a framed photo of him with Ty Dooley. "My best friend since third grade. He's in the navy."

"The two of you look like you could be brothers."

"Ty's like a brother." He was living the dream for both of them. Right now Ty was downrange somewhere classified. Caleb couldn't wait to see him again. "We planned on being in the navy together."

A grin spread across her face. "You wanted to follow in your grandfather's footsteps."

Caleb's muscles tensed. He'd never told anyone that except Ty. Becca guessing that made Caleb feel stripped bare and vulnerable. He didn't like it. He nodded once.

She studied him, her gaze sharp and assessing. "Military service is honorable, but you're following in your grandfather's footsteps by being Fair Face's CEO."

True, but Caleb felt no satisfaction. He'd wanted to be the kind of man his grandfather had been and nothing like his father.

Becca pointed to another photograph of Caleb with itty-bitty-bikini-clad supermodels clinging to him. "Most men would kill to be in your position."

He wasn't "most men."

The decision to run Fair Face had never been his to make. His worthless father hadn't wanted anything to do with the family company. To say that everything had fallen to Caleb was an understatement. He'd had to grow up fast. "What's the saying…? The grass is always greener."

"I wouldn't have expected that kind of longing from you."

Of course she wouldn't. But this—he glanced around the office—was never who he'd expected to be growing up. He'd dreamed about being a navy SEAL for as long as he could remember. Not the CEO of a skin-care company. "I'm sure there's something you wanted to be when you were growing up."

Becca nodded. "A vet. But I was a kid then. Very naive about how the world worked."

"Me, too," he said. "But that's what being a kid is all about. Dreaming of doing what sounds cool without understanding our places in the world."

"Too bad you couldn't trade jobs with your friend Ty for a week. Bet he'd enjoy hanging with supermodels while you swabbed decks on a ship or sub."

Caleb nearly laughed. An M4 rifle was more likely to be found in his best friend's hands, not a mop. Ty was one of the elite special ops guys, a navy SEAL, stationed in Virginia Beach on a Tier One team. Caleb would love a taste of Ty's life. "Fun idea, but I doubt I'd like swabbing decks."

"So you're more into adventure," she said. "Bet you'd like Special Forces kind of stuff. Best-of-the-best kind of thing."

Caleb didn't understand how she kept nailing him. He moved away from her. "What guy wouldn't?"

"Some might not, given the danger and risk involved, but I can see why it would appeal to you."

"Why is that?"

She tilted her chin. "The leadership skills you've honed as CEO would be useful even if the arena was different. Teamwork, too. No more profit margins, but life-or-death stakes. Kick-ass missions that would be more stressful than anything you've dealt with, but exciting due to the physical and mental challenges. You'd be surrounded by smart people. I'd assume someone who wasn't intelligent wouldn't last long, but in corporate America brainpower doesn't appear to be a prerequisite for rising to the top. At least here at Fair Face."

She might lack business experience, but she had what Grams would call gumption. "Not liking my grandmother's dog products doesn't mean employees here are stupid."

"Liking the products would prove they were smart." Becca stared at the photo of him and Ty again. "I think the real draw to your friend's lifestyle is loyalty. To the country, the service, your teammates. Heaven knows, you're loyal to your family."

Caleb couldn't move. Breathe. Blink.

How did she know this about him? A woman he'd known less than a week. One he'd underestimated.

"I suppose being in the navy would be more interesting work than sitting in meetings all day wondering what SPF of sunscreen would sell best," she added.

He found himself nodding.

"My only question is if joining the navy was so important to you, why didn't you enlist?" she asked.

"My family. Fair Face," he admitted. "They needed me."

"You wouldn't have been in the navy forever."

"No, but I was needed here. What I wanted to do…" He glanced at the photograph of Ty and him. "It was secondary."

Her eyes softened. "You love your family."

"Everyone loves their family."

"Not everyone would sacrifice their dreams."

Caleb shrugged, but the last thing he felt was indifference. He rubbed the back of his neck. He didn't want to have this conversation. He glanced at his watch, more out of habit than anything else. "It's getting late. I'll walk you to your car."

"Thanks, but that's not necessary," she said, a hint of a tremor in her voice. "My car is at the Park & Ride lot. I rode the bus into downtown."

"You took the bus?"

"Gas is expensive."

His grandmother had to be paying her a bundle, plus providing a free place for her to stay. Not to mention her job at the animal hospital. "You can't have money trouble."

She glared at him.

Forget daggers—Becca was firing mortar in his direction. He turned his hands palms up. "What?"

"I never said I couldn't afford it." Becca shot him a get-a-clue look. "Why should I want to waste my hard-earned cash to drive into town so you could try to get me fired?"

Stubborn. She also looked cute when she was angry. "Saving money is always good, especially when there's a motive or desire behind it. My grandfather taught me to save for a rainy day."

"Rain, thunderstorm, monsoon." Her fingers tightened around the strap of her messenger bag. "You never know what the future holds."

Caleb's life proved that was true.

"It's best to be prepared for anything." Well, almost anything. He hadn't been prepared for Becca. He should drive her home and see how deep her stubbornness ran. He shoved his laptop into his bag. "Come on, I'll walk you out."

CHAPTER SIX

WALKING ACROSS THE lobby of Fair Face's corporate headquarters, footsteps echoing on the tiled floor and questions swirling through her brain, Becca eyed the man next to her.

Caleb Fairchild looked like the perfect CEO in his gray suit—acted like one, too—but underneath the pinstripes was another man. A man who dreamed of adventure. A man who longed to serve his country. A man who sacrificed those dreams for his family.

Becca wondered if he ever let that side of himself show to anyone except his best friend. She would like to see it.

She'd been immune to pretty faces, charming smiles, killer eyes since the judge dropped the gavel in the courthouse in Twin Falls, Idaho. She went on occasional dates with working-class guys and cowboy types to have a little fun, but she always kept things casual. She was afraid of being burned again. She hadn't met anyone she'd wanted to get closer to. Getting closer to a guy made her vulnerable, a way she didn't like feeling.

Not that she wanted to get close to Caleb. But she had to admit the guy interested her. In a way she hadn't been interested in...well, forever. That was...a problem.

Her parents had a great marriage in spite of their financial struggles. But Becca knew finding a man who could accept her and her past wasn't going to be easy. Maybe that was why she hadn't been looking too hard to find "the one."

They passed another employee who was staying late that

evening. Caleb greeted him by name, the third in the past five minutes. "I hope you know how impressed we all were with those new label designs, Anthony. Great work."

The employee, an older man with gray hair and wire-rimmed glasses, walked away with a proud grin on his face and standing two inches taller.

"Do you know every single person who works here?" she asked.

"No, but everyone wears a badge," Caleb said. "That helps with the names."

Considerate of him, even though he'd accused her of trying to steal from Gertie. "The employees seem to appreciate your effort."

"They work hard." Caleb opened one of the double glass doors for her. "It's the least I can do."

"Thanks." His manners had impressed Becca the first time they'd met. She was impressed now in spite of his accusations. But she wouldn't allow herself to be taken in by him. Caleb Fairchild was no different from any other rich guy. She walked outside into bright daylight and stifling heat even though it was after seven at night. "The temperature hasn't dropped at all."

Two construction workers wearing paint splattered coveralls and carrying hard hats, walked toward them with tired smiles.

Caleb removed his suit jacket and draped it over his left arm. "Welcome to summer in Boise."

A fluorescent green food truck idled curbside with a line of customers waiting. The scent of garlic and rosemary filled the air. Becca's mouth watered. She stared at the plate of noodles and pork being dished up through the window.

"Hungry?" Caleb asked.

"A little." She hadn't eaten lunch. "Whatever they're cooking smells good."

"It does."

A siren wailed.

Goosebumps covered her skin in spite of the heat. She hated

sirens. The sound brought back too many memories, memories she wanted to forget.

Hearing the handcuffs lock around her wrists. Being shoved into a police car. Feeling the heartbreak of betrayal.

Becca crossed her arms in front of her chest and forced herself to keep walking.

She wished she could forget. She wished others could forget, too. She wished people would trust her.

Not just people. A person. Caleb.

The realization disturbed her as much as the siren.

Caleb's opinion didn't matter. And if she kept telling herself that she might finally believe it.

Stop thinking about him!

The sound faded into the distance.

With a deep breath, she lowered her arms then pointed to a white sign about ten feet in front of them. "This is where I catch the bus."

Caleb looked around at the few people waiting. "Let me drive you to the Park & Ride lot. I can follow you back to Grams's place and we can have dinner."

Becca's breath caught in her throat. She opened her mouth to speak. No words came out. She tried again. "Thanks, but there's no need for you to go to so much trouble."

"I need to eat, too." He whipped out his cellphone. "I'll see if Grams has eaten or not."

Dinner with Gertie, not a date with Caleb.

Becca should be relieved, not disappointed. The guy had serious doubts about her. He was everything she didn't want in a man. He was likely asking her to make amends for making her come here tonight. Of course, she'd never said yes to either the ride or dinner.

Caleb flashed his phone, showing her a text exchange. "Mrs. Harrison was going to warm something up for Grams, but she would rather have pizza. Does salad and a pepperoni pizza with mushrooms sound good?"

"Sounds great." The words escaped before Becca could

stop them. Darn, she knew better. On the bright side, Gertie would be thrilled to have her grandson there again and Becca wouldn't have to worry about making dinner tonight.

He typed on his phone. Messages pinged back and forth. "We're all set. Grams will have the pizza delivered."

Becca glanced at the bus stop, then looked at Caleb. "Back to Fair Face."

"My car is in the parking lot of the building next door," Caleb said.

"Gertie said there was parking available beneath Fair Face."

"There is."

This wasn't making sense. "Why aren't you parked there?"

"I prefer to let the employees and visitors use the closer spots."

Becca didn't want to be more impressed. She didn't want to like him, either. But she was. And she did in spite of a growing list of reasons she shouldn't. The guy took his responsibilities seriously.

She sneaked a peek at his profile. So handsome and strong and determined.

Maybe he took things too seriously.

A few minutes later, Caleb opened the door leading to a bank of elevators, blasting her with cool, refreshing air.

She stepped inside and waited for him to join her. "Please don't think you have to add me to your list."

"What list?"

"The list of people and things you have to take care of."

His eyes widened. His lips parted. Shock turned to confusion followed by a blank expression. "What do you mean?"

Maybe he was better at poker than she thought. If Becca hadn't been paying attention, she would have missed the play of emotion across his face. "Seems like you're the one responsible for taking care of your grandmother, your sister, Fair Face and your employees. I wouldn't want you to think I need taking care of, too."

"I didn't think that," he said. "You seem capable of caring for yourself."

She nodded. "But it makes me wonder."

"What?"

"Who takes care of you?"

His eyes clouded. His posture stiffened. "I take care of myself. I also know Ty has my six."

"Your friend in the navy."

"Best friend," Caleb said.

"I wish I had a best friend like that."

"You don't?"

"I haven't had a best friend since I was in seventh grade." Cecily Parker had lived in the trailer park for six months. The best six months of Becca's childhood. She and Cecily did everything together—rode the school bus, ate lunch in the cafeteria, had sleepovers. "Her mom met some guy online and moved to Cincinnati. Never heard from my friend again."

"What stopped you from getting a new best friend?"

"No one wanted to be friends with the kid who lived in the trailer park."

"You don't live in a trailer now."

"No, but making friends is different when you're older."

"That's true."

But some things hadn't changed.

Becca hadn't spent the last few years trying to get her life back together to make the same mistake again with Caleb. He wasn't Whit, but Caleb was rich, handsome and powerful, the kind of man who could get away with anything. The kind of man who wouldn't think twice about breaking her heart.

She needed to be smart about this, about him.

She'd agreed to a ride and dinner, but that was all. He could advise them. Help them. But keeping her distance from him would be her smartest move. Even if that was the last thing she wanted to do.

After dinner, Caleb walked out onto his grandmother's patio. Becca Taylor intrigued him. He didn't need a PhD to realize she didn't want to spend one more minute in his company.

Her not saying a word on the drive to the Park & Ride lot had been his first clue. The way she'd sat at the opposite end of the table, as far away from him as possible, had been his second clue. The way she'd scarfed down her pizza and salad, as if a bomb was about to explode if she didn't eat fast enough, and excused herself without wanting dessert had been his third and fourth clues.

No other woman had been so blatant in their dislike of him.

A door opened behind him.

"I thought you were heading home," Grams said.

Him, too. But something had stopped him from leaving. Not something. Someone. "I thought I might check on Becca first."

"She seemed preoccupied over dinner," Grams said.

He felt responsible. "Telling me what happened wasn't easy for her."

"But she did."

"Becca was very open about it." More so than he would have been if he'd been the one asked to explain.

"Do you still think she's trying to fleece me?"

You still have doubts.

Earlier this evening, the hurt in Becca's voice had sliced through him, raw and jagged and deep. But she was correct. He still had doubts. Becca was a stranger, an unknown quantity.

"People have ulterior motives and hidden agendas." Both his ex-fiancée and his mother, the definition of a gold digger, had had them. "That's human nature."

"Becca wouldn't hurt me or anybody."

Caleb wished he had Grams's confidence. But that was a lesson he should have learned from his father's mistakes. Instead, it had taken Cassandra to teach him that trust was something to be earned, not given freely to a stranger. "Maybe I'll feel that way after I get to know Becca better."

Though she knew him well enough. She understood him better than his family. Better than Cassandra. Better than everybody else in his life with the exception of Ty.

That bothered Caleb. If the wrong people knew too much, they could use that to their advantage. They could hurt you.

"I'm sure you will." Grams touched his arm. "It's getting late. Check on Becca, then head home."

"Will do." He hugged his grandmother. "And before I forget, thanks for the pizza and the cake."

Grams beamed. "This is your home. You're welcome anytime."

Being here brought back good memories and feelings of contentment. "Thanks."

Caleb followed the lighted path away from the patio. Stars filled the dark sky. Satellites circled above. The moon hung low.

A beautiful night. One he would have been spending alone in his loft working if not for Becca. Sure, he could have seen the sky from the twenty-foot windows, but he much preferred being here.

A cry filled the air. Not a human. A dog. In pain.

Adrenaline surged. Caleb broke into a run.

Becca.

The moans continued. Barking from other dogs, too.

Caleb knew it was a dog hurting, but his heart pounded against his ribs.

What if he was wrong? What if she was hurt?

He quickened his pace, his breath coming hard and fast.

Only the porch light was on at the guest cottage. He continued to the kennel.

The door was open, the lights on.

He ran inside.

Dogs stood at the front of their kennels barking and agitated.

He glanced around.

Becca sat on the floor, her legs extended. A stethoscope hung around her neck. She wore an ivory-colored lace-trimmed camisole that stretched across her chest. Her suit jacket covered the dog lying across her lap. The animal was the one who'd shed all over Caleb.

What was the dog's name? Morris?

No, Maurice. The Norwegian elkhound.

Caleb kneeled at Becca's side. Touched her bare shoulder. Ignored her soft skin and warmth beneath his hand. "What's going on?"

"Maurice." She rubbed the dog. "His stomach is distended. He's gassy and in pain."

The dog looked miserable. The other dogs wouldn't stop barking. Maurice wouldn't move.

"Is it serious?" Caleb asked.

"I don't know. I'm not sure what's wrong," she said. "The staff only uses products Gertie's made or approved, so I'm not worried about chemical poisoning. But if Maurice ate too much, there's the risk of bloat. His stomach could flip. Elkhounds aren't as prone as other breeds, but his pulse is high. Heart rate, too. I gave Gertie a call, but she didn't answer."

"She was on the patio with me."

"I'm going to take Maurice to the animal hospital where I work. I'd rather not take any chances."

Becca spoke calmly and in control, but worry filmed her eyes. He wanted to kiss it away. Hell, he wanted to make the poor dog feel better, too. "I'll let my grandmother know."

About to reach for his cellphone, Caleb realized he was still touching Becca's shoulder. He hadn't noticed. The gesture felt so natural, so right. Maybe because she was so different from other women he'd known, especially Cassandra. Maybe that was why Becca felt...safe. He lowered his arm then pulled out his phone.

"Tell Gertie not to worry," Becca said. "The door to the food cabinet door was ajar. Maurice might have gotten into there and gorged himself on whatever he found."

The dog released a groan that sounded as if someone was rolling his innards through a pasta machine.

The other dogs barked. Two howled.

Becca made soothing sounds and kept rubbing Maurice. "I bet you got into the food. Is that what happened, boy?"

The dog's gaze didn't leave hers.

Caleb thought that was one smart dog. Well, except for overeating.

"It's okay," Becca said. "You're not in trouble. Not at all."

Her soft voice was like a caress against Caleb's face, even though the words were for the dog's sake, he wished they were for him.

"You're going to have to go to the vet." She kissed Maurice's head. "You won't like that, but I'll be with you."

Caleb touched the dog. "I'll drive you."

"Thanks, but I've got a crate in the backseat. I need to move my car closer to make things easier on Maurice."

"I'll stay here with him while you do that."

"He'll shed on you."

"It's only dog hair," Caleb said. "And you have a lint roller."

The corners of her mouth curved in an appreciative smile. She stood. "Thanks. Be right back."

He took her place. The dog didn't seem to mind.

"It's okay, boy." He rubbed Maurice's head. "You're in good hands. Becca's going to take care of you."

Two brown, sad eyes met Caleb's. The look of total trust and affection sent the air rushing from his lungs. It was as if the dog understood.

Maybe Maurice did.

Caleb took a breath then leaned over so he could whisper in the dog's ear. "You're one lucky dog. I wish Becca liked me half as much as she cares for you."

But she didn't and wouldn't.

For the best, he told himself.

Too bad a part of him wasn't so sure.

Becca parked outside the kennel, left the engine idling then opened the car's back door.

Maurice was going to be fine. Just fine.

Repeating the words over and over again, she ran to the kennel.

If anything, she was wasting her time, gas and Gertie's money. Becca would be happy to waste all three as long as Maurice was okay.

She entered the kennel. Froze.

Caleb sat on the floor, in his designer suit, with Maurice's head resting on his lap. He rubbed the dog, talking in a soft voice.

Her mouth went dry.

The tenderness in Caleb's eyes as he stared at the dog sent Becca's heart thudding.

Her pulse rate kicked up a notch, maybe two.

Wait a minute. This was the same man who didn't trust her, who didn't like her, who wanted her fired.

But she couldn't help herself. He'd cranked up the charm without even realizing the affect this would have on her. Best to dial that down ASAP.

She cleared her throat. "How's he doing?"

"Not feeling too well, are you, boy?"

The sweet way Caleb spoke to the dog tugged at her heartstrings. Ignore it. Him. "Thank you for sitting with him. I can put him in his crate now."

Before Becca blinked, Caleb was on his feet. He picked up the dog easily, helping out both her and Maurice. "I'll carry him."

At the car, they loaded Maurice into the crate. She double-checked the latch to make sure it was secure. All set.

Caleb opened the driver's door.

"I appreciate your help." She hadn't known what to expect from Caleb, but his assistance with Maurice hadn't been it. "Tell Gertie I'll call as soon as I know anything."

"I'll check on the other dogs, then wait with Grams until you call. She wants to go with you."

"It could be a long night."

"That's what I figured," he said. "She opened the food cupboard to get dog treats earlier. She feels awful for not double checking the door was shut."

"Tell her not to worry. We'll get Maurice fixed right up."

"If not…"

"Let's not go there."

Their gazes met. Held. The same connection she'd felt the first day they'd met. But this wasn't the time to analyze things. Not with Maurice in pain.

Caleb kissed her cheek.

More of a peck, if she wanted to be technical, a brush of his lips over her skin. But her heart pounded. Warmth rushed through her.

"For luck," he said.

Becca resisted the impulse to kiss him back, only hard on the lips. She couldn't afford the distraction. Maurice needed her. She forced herself into the driver's seat then buckled her seat belt.

This wasn't the time or the place for more kisses. Most importantly this wasn't the man she should be kissing.

Not tonight. Not tomorrow night. Not ever.

Four hours later, Becca pulled into the guest cottage's driveway. Every muscle ached from tiredness. Her eyelids wanted to close. But she wasn't going to sleep much tonight.

Not when she needed to watch Maurice.

She glanced in the rearview mirror. "We're home, handsome."

The dog didn't make a sound. He must be exhausted after all the tests and X-rays. Not to mention his stomachache.

Becca grabbed her purse, exited the car and locked the door.

"Want a hand?"

Caleb.

He walked toward her, silhouetted by the porch light. He'd removed his jacket and tie, undone two buttons at the top of his shirt and rolled up his sleeves.

Her heart stumbled. "You're still here."

"I didn't want to leave Grams alone."

Becca wished she'd been the reason. Pathetic. But she was

pleased Caleb realized the difference between live-in staff and her grandson. "I hope she's not awake."

"She went to bed after you called."

"You should have gone home."

"It's fine." He spoke as if staying up half the night was no big deal. Maybe not for him, but she appreciated it. "Too bad the dog gorged himself on so many treats."

She nodded. "You should have seen the X-rays. Half his tummy was full."

"Last time he'll do that."

"Oh, no. He'll do it again if given the chance." Becca opened the crate's door. "Elkhounds will eat until they make themselves sick. They are food fiends. I knew something was wrong when he wouldn't eat his dinner."

Maurice lumbered out of the car as if each step hurt.

"Poor boy." Caleb picked up the dog. "Where do you want him?"

"On my bed," she said. "He's sleeping with me tonight."

"You really are a lucky dog."

Becca's cheeks heated. She was relieved for the darkness so Caleb couldn't see she'd blushed. "Not that lucky, considering the diet he'll be going on to get ready for the show this weekend."

Caleb was supposed to go, but he hadn't mentioned anything. Maybe he'd changed his mind.

She hoped not.

Wait a minute. That wasn't right. She didn't want him to go.

The cottage door was unlocked. She followed Caleb through the living room and into the bedroom. A sheet covered the comforter. Dogs spent so much time in here that cut down on her having to do laundry.

He gently set the dog on the bed. "Here you go, lucky dog."

"Thanks." She straightened the sheet then rubbed Maurice. "You should go. It's late."

Caleb's gaze narrowed on her. "You're exhausted."

"Long day. I'll sleep in a little while." She glanced at the dog who had curled up on her side of the bed. "I want to make sure he doesn't take a turn for the worse."

"Take a nap. I'll watch him."

A nap would be great, but she couldn't impose on Caleb. "That's nice of you to offer, but it's too late. You have to be at work in the morning."

"I'm the CEO," he said. "Grams won't complain if I show up late."

"This is *my* job."

Caleb tucked a strand of hair behind her ear.

A tremble ran through Becca. She didn't want to react to him, but couldn't help herself. He had a strange effect on her.

"It's mine tonight," he said.

A part of her wanted to let him take over, to not have to do everything herself tonight. She'd been on her own for so long with only herself to depend upon. But she couldn't...

Not when Caleb took care of so many others.

She raised her chin. "I'm not your responsibility."

"No, but how about we say you and Maurice are for the next couple of hours?"

The beat of her heart matched the quickening of her pulse. "You're making it hard for me not to like you."

His eyebrows wagged. "There's a lot to like."

His lighthearted tone made her smile. Something she hadn't thought possible at this late—make that early—hour. "Maybe, but it's hard to tell with dog hair all over you."

His mouth quirked. "You're covered in dog hair, too."

Becca didn't have to look to know it was true. "I'm always covered in dog hair."

"Grab some clothes." He kicked off his leather shoes. "Get comfortable on the couch."

"This is my bedroom."

"Not tonight." He crawled into bed with Maurice. The dog moved closer to him. "The boys have taken over."

"Are you always this bossy?" she asked.

"Yes," he said. "Get some sleep. Us boys will be fine. Won't we, Maurice?"

As if on cue, the dog licked Caleb's hand.

"See," he said.

Becca stared at him with a tingly feeling in her stomach. Funny—or maybe not so funny—but she could get used to "the boys" being here.

CHAPTER SEVEN

THLURP.

What was that? Caleb opened his eyes. Daylight filled the room. A mass of black and grey fur stood over him.

Thlurp.

A tongue licked his cheek.

He bolted upright.

Maurice's moist nose and his warm, smelly mouth were right in Caleb's face.

"Morning breath is one thing." Caleb turned away. "But yours is toxic."

The dog panted, looking pleased.

"At least you're up and about," Caleb said. "You must feel better."

Maurice stood on top of him. His paws pressed into Caleb's thighs.

"You're too big to be a lap dog."

The dog didn't listen. He plopped down, making himself at home on top of Caleb's legs.

"Okay," he relented. "You can sit here for a minute. But no longer."

"Are the boys having trouble this morning?" Becca asked.

The sound of her voice brightened his day like the first rays of sunshine through the window.

Caleb peered around the dog to see Becca standing at the foot of the bed.

She wore a pair of striped fleece pants and a tie-dyed ribbed tank top. Her hair was messy, as if she'd crawled out of bed or in her case, off the couch. Totally hot.

Waking up to Becca licking his face would have been much better. Too bad she couldn't join Caleb in bed now. He wasn't in the market for a relationship, but a fling would be fine. Fun.

Becca yawned, stretching her hands overhead.

His gaze shot to her chest, rising with her arm movement.

"You didn't wake me," she said.

He was staring. Gawking at her breasts. Not good. He looked at her face. "You were tired."

"So were you."

He'd checked on her in the middle of the night. She'd looked so peaceful with a slight smile on her face. He'd thought how appealing inviting her into bed with him would be. He'd imagined carrying her to bed. But that had bad idea written all over it. So he'd covered her with the blanket she'd kicked off and returned to bed with Maurice. "I wasn't."

"You stayed up all night."

"Not all night." Caleb's gaze kept straying to her tank top. "Once Maurice settled down, I dozed."

Becca moved closer.

The scent of her filled Caleb's nostrils. Wanting more, he breathed in deeper this time.

She touched the dog, leaning into him. Her hand brushed Caleb's thigh, sending shivery sparks up his leg.

"He looks better this morning," she said. "I'll take him outside."

"I took him outside around three."

Her lips parted, full and soft and kissable. If not for the dead weight on his lap, he would have tried to kiss her.

"I didn't hear you," she said.

"We were quiet." He glanced at the digital clock on the nightstand. "It's only five-thirty. Go back to bed."

"You're in my bed."

A sensual awareness buzzed between them.

A comfortable queen-size bed. A beautiful woman. A couple hours to kill until he was due at the office. This was looking pretty good.

"I'll scoot over. Maurice won't mind." Caleb moved closer to the far edge. It would be better if Maurice gave up his turn on the bed and went to the couch, but the dog didn't seem like the selfless type. Becca had that role locked up.

She watched him.

"The dog's on my side." Caleb kept his tone light, half-joking so he wouldn't scare her off. He patted the empty spot on the mattress. "Plenty of room for you now."

Her gaze shifted from him to the bed. "Better be careful, who you invite into bed, Mr. Fairchild."

"It's your bed."

"Then you should be even more careful. You wouldn't want to give away any corporate secrets over pillow talk."

He grinned. "Who said anything about talking?"

"You're full of surprises this morning."

He would be happy to surprise her more. All he needed was the opportunity and an invitation. "You're seeing only what you want to see."

"I'm seeing a pot and a kettle. Which one are you?" Amusement twinkled in her eyes. "I'd say the pot. But I suppose it doesn't matter, since they're both black."

Damn. Caleb shouldn't be so attracted to her. This went deeper than her looks. She challenged him, kept him on his toes. He liked that.

His ex-fiancée had always tried to suck up and sweet-talk him. Most women went along with him, rarely disagreed, as if he wanted a yes-woman instead of someone who spoke her mind and pushed his buttons.

Not that he wanted a woman. But he'd take this one for the morning. Hell, he'd stretch it to lunchtime if she were game. "That makes you the kettle."

"Works for me," she said. "I love kettle corn."

What was it about Becca Taylor that could get him turned on talking about cookware and popcorn?

Keeping his distance was the smart course of action if he wanted to avoid a complicated and messy situation. But leaving Becca's bed, especially if there was any chance of her climbing in it, didn't appeal to him in the slightest.

A fling would be fun. Easy. Safe.

And then Caleb remembered where he was....

The guest cottage at his grandmother's estate. With Grams's employee. His advisee.

A woman who made it hard to think straight when he was around her. A woman who knew too much about him. A woman who was the definition of dangerous.

Alarm bells sounded in his head. Maybe not so safe.

"It's all yours." Caleb moved the dog then slid off the bed. "I have to go."

"Okay." Becca bit her lip. "Thanks. Again. For, um, everything."

She looked as confused as he felt.

No matter. Time to get out of here before he changed his mind and did something really stupid, like trying to kiss the confusion out of her eyes.

Caleb patted the dog then slipped on his shoes. He tried to ignore how sexy Becca looked right now. "I need to put in extra hours at Fair Face with the dog show this weekend."

"You don't have to go." The words rushed out of her mouth faster than the rapids on the Snake River. "I can handle the show on my own."

She didn't want him to go. "I know, but I want to see about the products and my grandmother wants me there."

"Gertie is a worrywart when it comes to her dogs."

And when it came to Becca, too. Caleb was torn. As appealing as a weekend away from work sounded, spending more time alone with Becca wasn't smart. But he couldn't forget about his grandmother's wishes. "I'd rather not disappoint Grams."

"Gertie will understand if you're busy and have other plans." Becca's mouth tightened. "Say a date or something."

She'd baited the hook and cast the line. He didn't mind biting, if only to see her reaction and appeasing her curiosity about his going out with anyone. "No date. Work."

The lines around her mouth disappeared. "It's not a problem if you stay in Boise. Really."

"Well, since you don't mind…"

"I don't."

"I'll talk to Grams."

"Do."

She seemed too adamant about his not going. Maybe he'd misread her curiosity. Maybe she didn't want him to go to see what she'd be up to at the dog show. "I won't be around as much the next few days, possibly the entire week."

"Good. I mean…it'll be good to have time away. At Fair Face."

Becca sounded nervous. Flustered. She seemed so natural and unstudied and artless. Maybe he hadn't misread her after all.

A smile tugged at his lips. "Call me if you have any questions about the business plan."

"Will do. Thanks again for taking care of Maurice."

As if on cue, the dog jumped off the bed. He nudged Becca's hand with his nose so she'd give him attention.

Too bad that trick didn't work for Caleb. "You're welcome."

She bit her lip again. "You were on your way out?"

"Yes." Caleb grabbed his jacket and forced his feet to move in the direction of the front door. He'd better get going or he could end up staying here all morning. "Have a great day."

"Wait," she called out.

He stopped, hoping she was going to ask him to stay. A long shot, but this was as good a day as any to try being an optimist.

Becca handed him a lint roller. "Take this."

This was the last thing he expected. So much for optimism. Caleb laughed. "You need it."

"I have more than one, including two in my car."

"Always prepared."

"I never want to find myself unprepared again."

"I feel the same." He wasn't prepared for how much he wanted to stay with her now. Time to put some distance between him and the oh-so-appealing Becca Taylor "If I don't talk to you before the weekend, good luck at the dog show."

More than once after Caleb left the guest cottage, Becca picked up her cellphone to call Caleb. More than once she put away her cellphone.

That afternoon, she worked with Dozer on obedience training. The little guy needed to learn to behave and obey if he was ever going to find a forever home. Gertie would adopt him before sending him to live at the rescue shelter, but she and Becca agreed he'd do better with a family.

"Sit."

The dog sat.

"Stay."

She walked to the end of the leash, approximately six feet away, and hit the timer on her cellphone.

Dozer remained in place. Now to see if he sat for the full sixty seconds, a long sit in obedience training.

The seconds ticked off.

Becca wondered what Caleb was doing. He'd been on her mind since he'd left. She had questions about the business plan. As soon as she figured out one thing, that raised a bunch more questions. But she could find the answers herself if she searched on-line. The reason she wanted to call Caleb was to hear his voice.

Pathetic.

Hadn't she learned anything?

Even if Caleb was handsome, polite, hardworking, liked dogs, getting involved, at whatever level, with a man who had money was a bad idea. Like dumping water on an oil fire.

Explosive. She'd been burned once. No reason to repeat that experiment.

Stop thinking about him.

Becca needed to forget about Caleb and focus on getting ready to leave for the dog show on Thursday. She'd gotten her wish. She was going alone. If she needed a hand with the dogs, she could ask one of the Junior Showmanship kids to help her. Most of them were eager to help and learn more. She'd been that way.

Dozer rose to all fours and trotted toward her, as happy as a dog could be.

She glanced at the stopwatch. Forty-five seconds. Fifteen seconds too short. She gave him a pat. "We'll have to try this again.

Her cellphone buzzed. A new text message arrived. She glanced at the screen. From Caleb. Her hands tightened around the phone with excitement.

How's Maurice?

A ball of heat ignited deep within Becca. Caleb might have some faults, but he cared about the elkhound. She typed out a quick reply.

Good as new. Hungry again.

Maybe Caleb would find some spare time to stop by to see the dog. Maurice would like that. She would, too.

Becca waited for a reply. And waited. And waited.

She didn't hear from him. No texts. No phone calls. Nothing.

Tuesday gave way to Wednesday. Becca packed her suitcase and readied the RV for the trip to Central Oregon.

She tried not to think about Caleb. Or ask Gertie if she'd heard from him. He'd told Becca he wasn't going and would be busy. No. Big. Deal.

Thursday arrived. She packed everything she needed for the next three days in the RV.

Gertie said goodbye to each dog. "Don't cause Becca any trouble."

"They'll be fine," she said.

Gertie hugged her. The woman smelled like flowers and sunshine and the color pink. "Call me when you get there."

Becca loaded the dogs into their crates. "I will."

"I'm sorry you have to go alone."

"Caleb's a busy man." That was what she kept telling herself.

Concern filled Gertie's gaze. "Too busy. He's going to wake up one day and not have anything to show for it."

Becca thought a huge checking account balance would show for a lot, but she'd never had any money so what did she know?

Having so much responsibility thrust upon him at a young age had to have taken its toll. She wasn't going to add to his burdens. "Caleb will figure things out when he's ready. He's been spending more time with you."

"Last week, yes. This week, not so much. But you're right. Any time is an improvement. I just wish…"

"What?"

"I hate to think of you being alone this weekend."

"I'm not alone. I have the dogs to keep me company," Becca said. "I'll be fine."

The worry from Gertie's eyes didn't disappear. "I know. You're quite capable, but humor an old woman."

Becca's parents loved her. But they didn't have the luxury to sit around and worry about her the way Gertie did. Becca had been on her own from a young age because they'd worked multiple jobs. Knowing Gertie cared so much gave Becca a true sense of belonging. Something she hadn't found outside the trailer park or dog shows or the animal clinic where she worked. "How about I text you each time I stop to let the dogs out? I'll let you know what's going on during the show, too."

Gertie's features relaxed. "That would make me feel better."

Now, if Becca could stop thinking about Caleb and what he would be doing while she was away, she might feel better, too.

What the hell was Caleb doing here?

He glanced around the fairgrounds in Redmond, Oregon. White fenced outdoor show rings, dogs of every color and size, bright sunshine and green grass.

He was supposed to be working today, Saturday, not at a dog show. But Grams had said between showing the dogs and passing out samples of their dog products Becca had sounded exhausted and she still had two more days to go.

Caleb was responsible for so much. Now he had to take on his grandmother's dog consultant?

He could have said no to Grams insisting he attend. He could have sent someone else. But he'd wanted to see Becca.

If only Caleb could find her among the RVs, dogs, crates, grooming tables, rings and people. He'd tried calling and texting her, but couldn't reach her. He walked along the row of show rings.

On his left, vendors sold everything from dog-imprinted tea towels to doggy massage services. One booth had a dog tread-mill for owners who couldn't—didn't want to, perhaps?—take their animals for a walk. People passed out samples of food and treats. Seeing all these products first hand made one thing clear…Grams's skin care line didn't stand a chance against all the edible wares and dog-inspired tchotchkes.

He didn't see Becca anywhere.

Women and men dressed in business attire scurried around with combs, brushes, spray bottles and raced from the groom-ing stands to the ten show rings set up at the county fair-grounds.

Two big dogs barked at a group of smaller black-and-white papillons. Others from the show ring next to them joined in. Annoying, but they were dogs. Dogs barked and shed.

Outside the fenced area of Ring Six stood Becca. She wore a lime-green suit that showed off her curves nicely. She looked professional, as she had in his office on Monday night. But today she appeared more confident.

A puff of white stood at her side. Snowy must have spent his morning being bathed and primped to look like a cotton ball.

He walked toward her. Snowy saw him first and barked.

Becca turned. Smiled.

Her eyes widened. Twinkled.

Caleb's heart slammed against his ribs. He hadn't expected her to be so excited to see him. He'd thought she wanted him to be at the show, but her reaction told him otherwise. Maybe coming here hadn't been such a waste of time. "Hello."

"What are you doing here?" she asked, a breathless quality to her voice.

"Gertie said you sounded exhausted on the phone last night."

"What?"

"Grams said you were totally overwhelmed passing out samples and showing dogs and needed help."

Becca inhaled sharply. "So she sent you to the rescue."

He gave a mock bow. "At your service, milady."

"Thanks, but I have no idea why Gertie said what she did. I'm not overwhelmed or tired. Things are going well. I've passed out samples and feedback fliers. The interest has been high. Eighty percent of the people I've spoken with have taken the packages. I only have a few left."

"Then why am I here?" Though seeing Becca felt good. Thoughts of her had distracted him all week. He'd forced himself not to call her each day.

Becca scrunched her nose. "Gertie must have a reason."

But what? Grams never did anything without a reason. Well, except shopping. "Did my grandmother say anything to you?"

"Just that she hated the thought of my being here alone."

Alone. Alone. Alone.

The word echoed in his mind.

She didn't want Becca alone. Grams didn't want Caleb alone. She wanted them...

Together.

That would explain everything going on recently. "My grandmother's up to her old tricks."

"That's a relief," Becca said. "For a minute I was worried Gertie didn't trust me."

"That's not the case at all."

"So what's going on?

"Matchmaking."

"Matchmaking?" Lines creased Becca's forehead. Her mouth gaped. "With us?"

"It's the only thing that makes sense."

"I really don't think—"

"Can you come up with a better reason?"

"I…Well…" The startled look in her eyes matched the way he felt. "No, I can't."

"Grams has been vocal about wanting great-grandchildren, but I never thought she'd stoop to matchmaking." Caleb had to give Grams credit. She'd picked a woman who was the polar opposite of Cassandra. "But she created a line of baby products, so who knows how far she'd go?"

Snowy pulled away to sniff a small terrier, but Becca tugged on the leash stopping him.

"I don't think Gertie is playing matchmaker." Becca motioned to herself. "I'm not corporate trophy wife material."

Caleb took a long, hard look. "Don't sell yourself short. I like what I see."

"I'm not talking physical appearance." Her mouth slanted. "Imagine me schmoozing at a client party. Think about my past. I'm not the kind of woman you take home to meet your mother."

"My grandmother thinks you're amazing."

Becca straightened. A satisfied smile lit her face. "The feeling's mutual. But your grandmother is a special person."

"That's true." Becca's lack of pretense was far more appealing than the pretentious poise of his ex-fiancée and mother. "But you should know you're in a class so high above my mother it's not even funny."

Becca gave him a confused look. "Gertie said your mother died."

"She did, but if she were alive I would never want to introduce you to her. My mother married my father for his money. She ran off with her personal trainer. Once the divorce was finalized, we never saw or heard from her again."

Becca touched his arm. "What a horrible thing for a mother to do to her kids."

He shrugged. "Even before my mother deserted us, my grandparents were the ones raising us. It was them or a team of nannies."

"Sounds like you were better off with your grandparents."

He nodded, but this conversation was getting too personal. He'd never told anyone except Ty about his mom. Caleb wasn't sure why he'd shared the story with Becca. Maybe because she'd been so self-deprecating when she shouldn't have been. She was also easy to talk with.

Dogs continued barking. People milled about. Applause filled Ring Seven.

"When do you go?" he asked, changing the subject.

"After the Tibetan terriers."

"Snowy looks like a puffball."

"It takes time for him to be whitened, washed, volumized, combed, teased and sprayed."

"Do you do that with every dog?"

"Each breed is different," she said. "I have a schedule. I know who to work on when. Snowy's grooming is intensive, but he loves going in the ring, so he's more patient than some others. Maurice hates being on the grooming table. Blue doesn't mind it much."

A man in a suit and red striped tie approached. "Rebecca, isn't it?"

She nodded. "Hi, Dennis."

Caleb moved closer to her, unsure who this fellow was or why he seemed so interested in Becca.

Dennis smiled. "Nice job with the elkhound this morning. I thought you'd get Best of Breed."

"Thanks, but Gertie's happy with Select," Becca said. "This is Gertie's grandson, Caleb Fairchild."

"I'm Dennis Johnson." The man shook his hand, then looked right back at Becca. "Nice looking bichon. What products are you using on him?"

"Prototypes Gertie developed using all-natural, organic ingredients. I've been using them on all her dogs." Becca didn't miss a beat. "Would you like samples to try?"

The man looked as if he'd hit three sevens on a slot machine. "Yes, please."

"Find me at my RV. I have a package with the products and a form for you to give us your feedback."

"I'll be by later," the man said. "Good luck in the ring."

Caleb found the exchange interesting. The man recognized something different about the products Becca was using on her dogs. "Giving away samples with a feedback form is a good start, but maybe a little soon since you're not ready to manufacture products."

"Not on a large scale. But we can do something smaller in the interim."

"Sounds like Grams talking."

Becca nodded. "She's eager."

"More like a runaway train."

Which was why Grams playing matchmaker would mean trouble. Not only for Caleb, but Becca.

A woman in a purple apron walked past at a fast clip with an angry expression on her face. "That bitch didn't want to free stack."

Caleb waited for the woman to pass then looked at Becca. "That's…"

"Dog speak." Laughter filled her bright eyes. "I'm assuming you know that a bitch is a female dog. Stack means placing a dog in a position that shows off the breed standards. Hand stacking is when a handler manually positions the dog's paws.

Free stacking is when the handler uses bait, calls or signs to get the dog to position himself."

Dog showing didn't only have it's own vocabulary. A sociologist could have a field day studying these people and their interactions with each other and their dogs. But this was the most comfortable he'd ever seen Becca. Except at the kennel.

She adjusted the chain collar around Snowy's neck. "It's our turn."

A tall, thin man with a beard and in a three-piece suit called her number. Becca entered the ring with the dog. Three other handlers and their dogs, replicas of powder puff Snowy, followed them. The judge studied each of the dogs.

The dogs all looked the same to Caleb, but he couldn't take his eyes off Becca. She ran around the ring with Snowy, then positioned him in front of the judge. Caleb assumed that was hand stacking. They ran diagonally across the ring and back. One by one the other handlers did the same until all circled the ring in a line once again.

The judge pointed. Snowy won and was awarded a ribbon.

A few minutes later, Becca and Snowy returned to the ring and went through the same routine. Snowy was named Best of Breed, BOB for short, and Becca received a large ribbon.

Becca skipped out of the ring. "Gertie is going to be thrilled. I need to get Snowy in his crate so he can rest before Group, then I'll call…"

Caleb didn't know why her voice trailed off. "What?"

"Would you mind holding Snowy for a minute?"

He had no idea what was going on, but took Snowy's lead, a black leather leash with silver beads.

Becca walked twenty feet away to a little girl, who looked to be around seven or eight. The child sat on a folding chair. She held the leash of an Irish setter puppy with both hands and wiped tears from her face with her arm.

"Hello, I'm Becca." She knelt at the girl's side and put her hand in front of the dog nose. "What's your name?"

"Gianna."

"You have a pretty dog."

Gianna hiccupped. "Thank you."

Caleb had no idea what Becca was doing, but moved closer so he could find out.

The dog sniffed her hand. "What's your puppy's name?"

"P-Princess."

"Is Princess going to be shown today?"

"No." Gianna sniffled. "My mommy twisted her ankle, so can't show her. This would've been Princess's first time in the ring."

Becca looked around. "Where is your mommy?"

"Getting ice for her foot."

"When your mom gets back, why don't we ask if she'd let me show Princess for you."

Gianna's tears stopped flowing. Her mouth formed a perfect O. "You're a handler?"

Becca petted the dog, and Gianna scooted closer to her. "I'm a dog handler and I'd be happy to show Princess."

Caleb knew Becca had a full schedule, especially with Snowy continuing on, yet she wanted to help this little girl.

Becca's action filled him with warmth. How many people had walked past the crying child without noticing or pretending not to see her? But she'd done something about it. The woman was…special. He couldn't believe he'd doubted her motivations and accused her of being a scam artist.

A thirtysomething woman with her hair in a bun and wearing a purple suit hobbled toward them. She carried a plastic bag full of ice. "Gianna?"

The girl leaped out of her chair. She bounced from foot to foot, her ponytails flying up and down. "Mommy, Mommy, this lady can show Princess for us. She's a handler."

Becca rose and held out her hand. "My name is Becca Taylor. Your daughter told me about your ankle. I'd be happy to show your puppy for you."

"Oh, thanks." The woman's gaze flitted from Becca to her

daughter and the dog. "That's nice of you to offer, but I can't afford to pay for a handler."

"No charge," Becca said without any hesitation. "I wouldn't want Princess to miss her first time in the ring."

Caleb's chest tightened, a mix of affection and respect, at her generosity. One more attribute to add to Becca's growing list. But she wasn't being a smart businesswoman, given her first priorities were Grams's dogs and the product samples. He assumed Grams wouldn't mind, given her kind heart, but even if she did, Caleb wasn't about to say a word. Becca was doing exactly the right thing.

Gianna tugged at her mother's arm. "Please, Mommy. Please, oh, please, oh please."

The woman looked stunned. Relief quickly took over. "Th-that would be great. Thank you."

Becca glanced back at Caleb. "Do you mind holding unto Snowy a little longer so I can work with Princess?"

"Happy to." He would do whatever she asked. She was so genuine he wanted to help her, not make things harder. "I'll put him into his crate."

"That would be great."

"Come on, Snowy." If Caleb hurried, he might make it back to watch her in the ring. "I don't want to miss this."

But whether Becca Taylor was in the ring or out of it, she was a very special woman. There was no other place he'd rather be this weekend than right here with her.

CHAPTER EIGHT

BECCA STOOD OUTSIDE the ring where Best in Show, aka BIS, would be held in a few minutes. She wiggled her toes inside her black flats. The dogs, including Princess, had all placed in their events and Snowy had won his group. The buzz surrounding Gertie's dog-care samples kept increasing. Gertie was beside herself with pride. Win or lose in the next few minutes, the day couldn't get much better.

"You look so calm and cool." Caleb stood next to Becca. "Not the least bit nervous."

She glanced his way. Her stomach did a somersault. She was so happy he was here.

"I'm more excited than anything else." Becca wanted to pinch herself to make sure her eyes were open and she wasn't dreaming. She adjusted Snowy's lead in her hand. "No matter how Snowy does, we've already won. People are very interested in Gertie's new line of dog products."

"It can't hurt your reputation, either."

"Or Snowy's. He's on his way to Grand Champion," she said. "But he's never won BIS."

"Today could be the day."

Caleb's words, spoken with sincerity, pierced her heart like an arrow. She double-checked Snowy to make sure he looked his best, then rerolled his lead. "I hope so."

"Good luck." The tender look in his eyes made her feel as

if they were the only two people at the fairground. Her breath caught. Her temperature rose. "Not that you need luck."

Her heart melted. If only he'd wished her luck with a kiss the way he had when she took Maurice to the vet on Monday night.

Caleb's gaze lingered, tenderness turning to something resembling desire.

Her pulse skittered. He might want to kiss her again.

Please, oh, please. She realized she was acting like a little girl, like Gianna.

Becca didn't care. She parted her lips, in case he was looking for an invitation.

Then she realized…they weren't alone. Hundreds of people stood and sat ringside, many who knew Gertie. Going down this path with Caleb was fruitless and dangerous. He might have decided Becca wasn't a scam artist, but a kiss would mean nothing to him. A kiss would mean more to her. Kissing him, even if she might want that, wasn't right or smart or even sane.

She was about to go in for Best of Breed. She needed to concentrate on Snowy, not think about Caleb.

Becca pressed her lips together.

The ring steward announced the competition.

She took a deep breath and raised her chin.

"You're going to kill them," Caleb whispered, his warm breath against her ear. "No one stands a chance against you and Snowy."

His words provided an extra jolt of confidence. Not needed, but nice. Very nice, actually.

She fell in line with the six other handlers and their dogs.

With a grateful smile in his direction, Becca squared her shoulders, then stepped into the ring with Snowy.

It was show time!

Best in Show!

Snowy—registered name White Christmas in Sunny July—had been awarded Best in Show.

Pride flowed through Caleb. His chest expanded with each breath. A satisfied smile settled on his lips.

The crowd applauded and cheered.

He videotaped the award ceremony. Snowy pranced around as if he knew he was top dog, but Becca's wide smile and joy-filled eyes defined the moment for Caleb. A photographer snapped official winner pictures with the judge. Handlers shook Becca's hand. She juggled the gift basket, flowers and three feet long ribbon she'd been awarded.

Caleb stood back, away from the entrance to the ring, and waited. He wanted to watch Becca savor the win.

People congratulated her on the way out of the ring, but she gave all the credit to Snowy, who soaked up the attention as if he knew he'd be getting extra doggy treats tonight. Little Gianna and her mom hugged Becca.

The crowd dispersed.

Becca made her way to him, her arms extended outward with the basket and flowers and Snowy's leash and ribbon in the other. "Best in Show!"

"Congratulations." Caleb wrapped his arms around her. Her breasts pressed against his chest. The feeling of rightness nearly knocked him back a step. Holding her felt good, natural. He didn't want to let go. He chalked it up to working too hard on the baby product launch and not going out on many dates. He forced himself to drop his arms. "You killed it."

She blushed, a charming shade of pink. "Thanks, but Snowy did all the work."

Becca was too modest. But that was something he liked about her. "We need to celebrate. Bend has some nice restaurants."

"Thanks, but I don't want to leave the dogs alone in the RV."

The dogs. He'd forgotten about them even though he couldn't look anywhere without seeing one dog or twelve. "We can find a place that delivers."

"I'm all set for food for the weekend. I never leave the grounds of a show once I arrive," Becca said. "I'm positive

Gertie will want to celebrate when we're home. She's never had a dog win Best in Show. She'll probably throw a party."

"Sounds like Grams." But Caleb didn't want to wait. He wanted to make tonight special for Becca. "But we can still celebrate here."

"I thought you were going to fly home tonight. Don't you have to get to the airport?"

"I was…am." But Caleb wasn't sure he wanted to leave now. "Unless you want me to stay."

"Don't waste your entire weekend here. Fly home so you and your sister can have brunch with Gertie."

Caleb did that every Sunday. He would rather have brunch with Becca. Preferably after spending the night together. The idea of having a fling with her had been floating around his head since he saw her standing next to the bed Tuesday morning.

She juggled the items in her arms.

He took the basket and flowers from her. "I've got these."

"Thanks." A smile brightened her face. She walked with a playful bounce to her step. Neither of which he had anything to do with.

He wanted to be the reason she was so happy, but only dogs got that honor. He was at a disadvantage without four legs and fur.

The light fragrance of the flowers tickled his nose, teasing him, as if the blossoms knew he wouldn't be around in the morning, but they would be.

People streamed out of the fairgrounds. Engines roared to life. Horns honked. Dogs barked. People were clearing out, returning to their hotels off-site. Others returned to their RVs parked in a special area at the fairgrounds.

Becca placed Snowy into his pen under the shade of an awning then checked the other dogs. "Want a drink or a snack before you head to the airport?"

"What makes you think I'm leaving now?"

Her eyes widened. "I assumed you'd want to get home."

"Home is a three-thousand-square-foot loft in downtown Boise." A quiet place—a lonely place—compared to the activity and noise here. He breathed in the fresh air. "This is a nice change. No need to rush back."

"You're more than welcome to join me for dinner. I'm grilling hot dogs."

He did a double take. "Hot dogs."

"Does wiener dogs work better? Or how about Dachshund dogs?" she teased. "We're at a dog show. A themed meal makes sense."

"What else is on the menu?"

Laughter filled her eyes. "Saluki Slaw, Bloodhound Beans and Pekinese Potato Chips. Oh, and Corgi Cookies for dessert."

"Corgi cookies, huh?"

"There's also Bernese Brownies."

A quick thinker. He liked that. "Not a bad job coming up with those names on the fly."

And turning a meal into fun. He needed to have more fun.

"Not bad." A corner of her mouth slid upward. "Darn good if you ask me."

"You've convinced me to stay. I'll fly back to Boise after dinner so I can still have brunch with Grams in the morning."

Panic replaced the laughter in Becca's eyes. She shot him a what-have-I-gotten-myself-into smile. She tugged her bottom lip with her teeth. "Win-win."

She was a good sport. "Those are the games I like."

Except he wasn't sure what he was doing with Becca right at this moment. There was no reason for him to stay and every reason in the world to go. Hot dogs weren't his typical Saturday night dinner fare, but he was more interested in the company, Becca's company. And, how could he turn down a Corgi cookie?

Win-win any way he looked at it.

After dinner, Becca stood at the RV's sink. She placed the paper plates and plastic utensils from dinner in the garbage.

She kept a smile on her face, but tension wreaked havoc inside her. Awareness of Caleb flowed down her spine and pooled at her feet. She slanted a glance over her shoulder. "I'm almost finished."

Caleb sat in one of the leather lounge chairs. His legs were extended and crossed at the ankles. His gaze on her. "You'd be finished if you'd let me help."

Cleaning up after dinner gave her something to do with her hands other than combing her fingers through her hair and straightening her clothes. Being around Caleb made Becca self-conscious about her appearance, about everything. It wasn't anything he did—he offered to help prepare the meal and clean up. Or anything he said—he was easy to speak with and complimentary. It was just…him.

She placed the now-dried pans in the cabinet above. "There wasn't much to do."

"Maybe not in the kitchen," he said. "What about the dogs?"

She checked the clock on the microwave. "I need to take them for walks."

Caleb rose. "I'll go with you."

"What about your flight?"

He took a step toward Becca. His tall, athletic frame made the spacious and luxurious RV feel like a pop-up trailer. "It's Grams's jet. There's no set departure time until I tell them I'm ready."

"Must be nice." Becca was still trying to get used to Gertie's top-of-the-line RV, purchased specifically for dog shows. She held out a plastic container containing the leftover cookies. "Want more?"

"If I eat another bite, I'll need a crane to get me out of here." He patted his flat stomach. "I forgot how good hot dogs tasted."

"Must be a big change from the haute cuisine you eat."

"Prime rib is about as fancy as I get," he said. "I take after my grandfather when it comes to food. Gramps was a meat-and-potatoes man. Much to the chagrin of Grams, who liked to experiment in the kitchen the way she does in the lab. We usually ended up with two dinners when I was a kid. One for Gramps that our cook made and one for the more adventurous appetites that Grams provided."

"Which did you eat?"

"Both. I took one bite of whatever Grams cooked. Sometimes more. Only once did I spit it out. I made her promise never to tell me what it was."

"Growing up with Gertie must have been interesting."

"It was never boring. But no matter how busy my grandparents were with Fair Face, we always ate dinner together. That was our special time."

"Sounds nice." She felt a twinge of envy, even though she knew she'd been loved. "My parents worked multiple jobs so eating meals together didn't happen much."

"That had to have been rough."

"It's all I knew." She put the lid on the cookies, then set the container on the counter. "My folks worked hard to make ends meet so it was difficult for me to complain."

"You get your work ethic from your parents."

She nodded. "I wish things were easier for them. Maybe someday…"

"Invite them to visit you at Grams's house."

"Gertie suggested that, but my parents don't have the same days off," Becca said. "I emailed them pictures. They thought the estate looked like something from a TV show. The grounds impressed my dad. His dream is to have a lawn to mow."

"We've always had gardeners to take care of that, but I thought the rider mower looked fun."

"I take it your loft doesn't have a yard."

"No. There's a terrace with planters and a lap spa. Grass would be impractical."

She exited the RV. Caleb followed her out. The sun had disappeared beneath the horizon. Street lamps along the roads that now doubled as walkways around all the RVs lit up the area.

"Well, if you ever want a lawn up there, there's always Astroturf"

He gave her a look. "You can't mow Astroturf."

"Vacuum it."

"Vacuuming doesn't sound like fun."

"Let me guess—you've never vacuumed."

"I haven't."

Their lives were so different. Too different. She couldn't forget that even if she liked talking and being with him and wondering what kissing him would feel like. "Try it sometime. Vacuuming is a good way to clear your mind."

"Maybe I will."

She locked the RV door. "Maybe means you won't."

A sheepish grin spread across his face. "Wouldn't want to offend the team that cleans my place."

Whoa. He lived in a completely different universe than her. "You have a team of cleaners?"

"Doing my part to stimulate the economy."

Okay, that was funny. She liked his sense of humor. With a smile, she shook her head. "Working for Gertie sure has given me a glimpse into how the other half lives."

"What do you think so far?"

His question didn't sound flippant, but why would he care what she thought? Few people except her parents and Gertie did.

"That bad, huh?" he asked.

"No, not at all."

"So…"

He sounded genuinely interested in knowing Becca's opinion. "Honestly, it's been nice," Becca said. "Gertie is eccentric and loves luxurious things, but she's more grounded than I imagined someone as wealthy as her to be. It'll be hard to leave behind."

His gaze narrowed. "Planning on going somewhere?"

"Not in the near future, but I want to be a full-time handler. Care for the dogs in between shows. Teach handling classes to kids and dog owners."

"You can make a living doing that?"

His disbelief didn't surprise her. "The top handlers in the country make over six figures a year."

"I had no idea people did this as a full-time job."

"A few do," she said. "Most work other jobs and handle part-time or as a hobby. Some save money so they can take time off."

"Saving for a rainy day."

She couldn't believe he remembered their conversation in his office. "Yes."

"You realize you could have a lucrative career working for Grams, especially if the dog-care products take off. You'd earn more than you'd make as a dog handler."

Becca shrugged. "I never set out to be a business person."

"You care about what you do. You're not just out to make a buck."

"No, but having a few bucks in the bank doesn't hurt."

He smiled. "You belong here. In this dog-show world."

"I think so." She hoped this was where she belonged. "I appreciate Gertie giving me the opportunity to show her dogs."

Becca attached Maurice's leash to his collar and released him from the pen. The dog ran straight to Caleb.

"You have a new friend," she said.

He rubbed the dog's head. "It's only because I have no dog hair on me. Maurice needs to mark his territory."

"As long as he's not marking it another way."

Caleb gave her a look. "Don't give Maurice any ideas."

Becca peeked in on Snowy. The dog slept soundly, his back leg jerking as if dreaming. She would take him out later.

"Come on, Blue." She removed the gray eighteen-month-old puppy from his pen. "Time for your walk, boy."

Caleb walked next to her with the dogs out in front, leading the way.

A man, a well-known handler from California, walking four beagles, greeted them with a nod and a hello.

Caleb looked back at the dogs. "Some people show the

same type of dogs. Why doesn't my grandmother stick to one breed?"

"Gertie loves all dogs, not a particular breed. She also owns dogs others weren't sure about or gave up on. She could have the pick of most litters, but she'd rather choose a dog who needs a second chance."

"Why would they need a second chance? They're pure-breds."

"Yes, but not every purebred meets the breed standard. Reputable breeders have those dogs neutered or spayed and placed in homes as pets." Becca pointed to Blue. "This guy was the runt of the litter. No one expected him to be show quality, but your grandmother saw something in him and took a chance. Now he's on his way to being a champion."

"I'm not surprised," Caleb said. "Grams has always been fond of strays."

"No kidding. She took me in."

"My sister and me, too."

"You weren't strays," Becca countered. "You're family."

Caleb shrugged.

"Gertie treats her rescue and foster dogs the same as her show dogs." Becca could tell he didn't want to talk about this. "Your grandmother has a big heart."

"So do you."

His words meant more than they should. Becca tried to down play the fluttery feeling in her stomach. "It's easy with dogs."

"There was that little girl Gianna today."

"Just trying to be nice."

"Is that what you're doing now? Being nice to me when you wish I'd left hours ago?"

Becca didn't know what she was doing. Feeling. But she didn't like how Caleb saw right through her, as if her every thought and emotion were on display especially for him. They were too much in sync, able to understand each other even though they were in very different places in life.

He made her feel vulnerable, a way she'd felt for three long years in prison. A way she never wanted to feel again. She tightened her grip on the leash and looked up at the sky full of twinkling dots of lights. "Lots of stars out tonight."

"You're changing the subject."

"You're supposed to pretend you don't notice and play along."

He stopped walking to allow Maurice to sniff the grass. "What if I don't want to do that?"

"You're the kind of guy who plays by the rules."

"Normally, yes." He moved closer to her until she could feel the heat of him. "But this isn't normal."

She fought the urge to step back. "Being at the dog show?"

Caleb stopped inches away from her. "Being here with you."

The light from the streetlamp cast shadows on his face. He looked dark and dangerous and oh-so-sexy. Becca swallowed. Last time she'd thought that about a guy she'd ended up in jail. That might not be what would happen to her next, but she shouldn't take any unnecessary chances and do something stupid again.

His gaze locked on hers. "Do you want to keep playing by the rules?"

Her heart slammed against her ribs. She should step back. Way back. Put distance between them. For her own good. And his.

But her feet wouldn't move. She remained rooted in place, waiting, hoping, anticipating.

Caleb tilted his head down, bringing his lips close to hers.

Becca rose up and leaned forward.

Their lips touched.

So much for rules.

He wrapped his arms around her, pulled her close and kissed her hard.

Hot, salty, raw.

His lips moved across her, skillfully. His kiss possessed, as if staking a claim and declaring she was his.

Becca had never felt that way before. She shouldn't like it, either. She was independent. She didn't need a man to give her value. But at the moment, with tingles reaching to the tips of her toes and fingers, possession seemed a small price to pay.

Pleasurable sensations pulsed through her, heating her from the inside out. He deepened the kiss. She followed willingly, arching toward him.

Ruff.

Caleb jerked backward. His arms let go of her.

Becca stumbled to the right.

Grrrrowl.

Maurice and Blue lunged toward two teeth-baring Pekingese with satin bows on their ears.

She yanked on the leash. "Heel!"

Caleb grabbed Maurice by his collar.

The other two dogs didn't back down. Their owner, a petite woman with spiky white hair, a shimmery short robe and flower-trimmed flip-flops, frowned. "Next time get a room."

Becca's cheeks burned. Her lips throbbed.

Oh, no. She'd been so wrapped up in Caleb she had forgotten about the dogs. What if they'd gotten into a fight and been hurt? Not acceptable.

The woman marched away, dragging her wannabe fighters behind her. The dogs looked back and growled.

"That didn't turn out like I expected. Maybe Grams knows something we didn't." Desire flared in his eyes. "We should try that again."

Oh, yes. Becca would love another kiss. Make that kisses. But she couldn't. She glanced at Blue, who sniffed the grass as if nothing had happened. If only she could forget…The past. Who Caleb was. Who she was. "I can't."

"Can't or won't?"

"Does it matter?

His jaw was set, tense. "If not for those bow-toting dogs—"

"If it weren't for them, I'd still be kissing you."

A sinfully charming grin lit up his face. "Then let's pick up where we left off."

Temptation flared. "Kissing you was…amazing. But I forgot everything, including the dogs. They could have been hurt. They're my responsibility. I can't be distracted."

Approval tempered the desire in his gaze. "I understand and respect that."

Respect was all she'd wanted. Until this moment. Now she wanted more of his kisses. Uh-oh.

"Thanks." She tried to remember all the reasons Caleb and more kisses weren't good for her. "I appreciate it."

"Just know when you're back in Boise and the dogs aren't around, I want to kiss you again. If that's what you want, too."

Her heart lodged in her throat. She couldn't breathe, let alone speak.

Heaven help her, but Becca couldn't wait to get back to Boise.

CHAPTER NINE

TWO NIGHTS LATER, the party at Grams's place was going strong when Caleb arrived. He handed his keys to a parking valet.

A big crowd for a Monday.

But when Gertie Fairchild issued an invitation, few sent regrets.

Inside the house, Caleb greeted people he'd known his entire life and made his way toward the patio.

Leave it to Grams to pull together an impromptu gathering for two hundred of her closest friends in honor of Snowy winning Best in Show. On the patio, a DJ spun music in the backyard. Bartenders fixed drinks. Uniformed servers carried trays of delicious smelling appetizers.

Caleb searched for the two women he wanted to see most—his grandmother and Becca. He caught a glimpse of Grams, wearing pink capris and a sparkly blouse, and wove his way over through the crowd.

"Caleb!" Grams hugged him. "I've been wondering when you'd arrive."

"I had a few things to finish up at the office."

"Take off your jacket and tie," she said with a smile. "Get a drink. And relax."

He glanced around.

"Looking for Becca?" Grams asked.

"Yes."

"She's here. Courtney, too."

His sister never turned down a party invitation, even if the average age of the guest list was twice hers. "I hope Courtney's staying out of trouble."

"Probably not." Grams waved at someone who'd stepped out onto the patio. "You should find Becca and see if you can get yourself into trouble."

"Grams!"

"What?" She feigned innocence. "Thirty-one is too young to be so serious about everything. Becca would be good for you. Help you to lighten up and enjoy life."

Maybe in the short term. He'd enjoyed their time together at the dog show. Talking, laughing, kissing. Best not let Grams know or she'd be hiring a wedding planner to come up with the perfect proposal, one that would go viral on YouTube. "Becca and I figured out you've been playing matchmaker."

Grams pointed to herself. *"Moi?"*

"Oui, Grandmère."

"Speak French to Becca," Grams said. "Women like that."

Caleb shook his head, but made a mental note to give speaking French a try.

"Becca is a special woman." Grams lowered her voice. "But it's going to take a special man to break through her hard shell."

"Becca and I are friends." Friends who had shared a passionate kiss before being rudely interrupted by a pair of Pekingese dogs. He might want more of Becca's kisses, but he wasn't that "special man." The last thing he needed was a girlfriend. He didn't want to be responsible for one more person. "Nothing more."

"Your loss is another man's gain."

The thought of Becca kissing another man made Caleb's shoes feel too tight. He stretched his toes. "I'm going to see if I can find Courtney."

"Have fun." Grams flitted toward the house, taking on her role as Boise's most gracious hostess.

Caleb grabbed a bottle of beer from the bar. He took a long

swig. Just what he needed after a long day at the office. Now, if he could find Becca.

"Hey, bro." The scent of his sister's perfume surrounded him. Her ruffled miniskirt barely hid her underwear. Her two tanks showed as much skin as a string bikini top. Her blonde hair was clipped on top of her head with tendrils artfully placed around her face. Her make up was magazine layout perfect. Typical Courtney. Somewhat disturbing for a brother who worried about his younger sister. "I met your new girlfriend."

He nearly spit out his beer. He forced himself to swallow. "I don't have a girlfriend."

"Becca."

"She's not...What has Grams been telling you?"

"Only that she found the perfect woman for you." Courtney took a flute of champagne from the tray of a passing waiter. "Becca is cute. With a wardrobe makeover, some highlights and makeup she could be totally hot. I'm happy to assist—"

"Becca is fine the way she is."

"You like her."

"I don't..." He lowered his voice. "Becca is sweet. She doesn't need to be pulled into Grams's matchmaking scheme."

"Better her than me." Courtney sipped her champagne. "The alarm on Grams'a great-grandbaby clock is ringing louder and louder."

"Don't look at me. I do enough as it is."

"Well, I'm not ready to be a mom. I've never dated a guy longer than a month."

Caleb stared at her over the top of his beer bottle. "Considering your choice in men, that's a good thing. Maybe you should have Grams fix you up. Bet she'd pick a winner for you."

"Yeah, right. Someone totally respectable, proper and boring like you." Courtney shook her head. "Don't forget I lose everything. Imagine if I misplaced a kid. That would be bad."

"Very bad," he agreed. "No worries. Grams will get over the idea of great-grandchildren eventually."

"I hope so, but I think we should be proactive about this," Courtney said. "Let's buy Grams a kitten."

"Grams is a dog person."

"That doesn't mean she can't be a crazy cat lady, too. Kittens are cute and cuddly. Kind of like a baby, but you don't have to deal with diapers, only litter boxes."

Caleb wasn't in the mood to try to understand his sister's twisted logic, especially after she'd called him boring. He downed what remained of his beer. "Hold off on the kitten for a while. And stay out of trouble tonight."

Courtney stuck her tongue out at him. "You're no fun."

Walking away, he realized Courtney was correct. He used to be fun. When he was younger, he and Ty had had nothing but fun. After Caleb took over Fair Face for his grandfather, life revolved around the company and family. Nothing else.

He followed the path past the guest cottage—only the porch light was on—to the kennel.

A dog barked from inside.

Caleb couldn't see which one, but he recognized the sound. Maurice.

Caleb entered the kennel. More barks erupted, drowning out the pop music playing from an iPod docking station.

"Quiet." Becca faced Dozer's door. Her floral skirt fell two inches above her knees. The green sleeveless shirt showed off toned arms. Her white sandals accentuated thin ankles. "We don't want Gertie's guests to hear you."

The dogs stopped barking. Maurice stood with his front paws on his door.

"What's gotten into you?" Becca asked the dog.

Caleb stopped two feet behind her. "So this is where you've been hiding."

She gasped and whirled around.

The hem of her skirt flared, giving him a glimpse of her lower thighs. Much more enticing than a super short skirt that left nothing to the imagination.

Her eyes were wide, her cheeks pink. She placed her hand over her heart. "Caleb."

"I didn't mean to startle you."

She peered around him, as if to see if anyone else was behind him. "What are you doing here?"

"I was going to ask you the same question." Seeing her felt good. He couldn't believe they'd only been apart two days. It seemed longer. "The party's up on the patio. But you're down here. Alone."

She motioned to the dogs, watching them intently from their individual stalls. "I'm not alone."

"You know what I mean."

She nodded. "It's a bit...overwhelming."

"The party?"

"And all the people. Guests, servers, bartenders, DJ, parking valets," she said. "Gertie introduced me to about a hundred people tonight. No way can I keep the faces and names straight."

"So you escaped here."

Another nod. "This is my favorite place at the estate. It's where I'm..."

"Comfortable," he finished for her.

"Yes. It's where I fit."

The way he knew her, understood her was...unsettling to him.

He cut the distance between them in half with one step. "You love the kennel and the dogs, but you also fit in up at the house with everybody else."

She ground the toe of her sandal against the floor. "I don't know about that."

"I do." Caleb used his finger to raise her chin. "You're smart, beautiful, kind."

The pink on her cheeks darkened. "You don't have to stop."

"I don't plan on stopping unless you want me to stop." He didn't want to frighten her off "I'd like to pick up right where we left off."

Her lips parted.

He grinned. "I'm going to take that as an invitation."

"Please."

Caleb kissed her. Something he'd been thinking about doing since he drove away from the fairgrounds on Saturday night. But he never expected her to melt into his arms as if she'd been looking forward to this moment as much as him.

He pressed his lips against hers, soaking up the feel and taste of her.

So sweet. Warm. His.

He wrapped his arms around her, pulling her close. She went eagerly. Her soft curves molded against him.

So right.

His temperature shot up, fueled by the heat pulsing through him.

Her hands were on his back, in his hair, all over.

His tongue explored her mouth, tangled with her tongue. He couldn't get enough of her.

Caleb's hand dropped to her skirt. He lifted the hem and touched her thigh, the skin as soft and smoothed as he imagined. His hand inched up, with anticipation, with desire.

"Well, I'll be damned."

Grams.

He jerked his hand from underneath Becca's skirt. He jumped back totally turned on, his breathing ragged. Becca's flushed face and swollen lips were sexy as hell and exactly the last thing he wanted his grandmother to see.

Too late now. He faced the woman who had raised him. Courtney stood next to his grandmother.

Grams had her hands clasped together. She looked giddy, as if she'd been granted three wishes from a magic lamp. She needed only one, because the silly grin on her face told him exactly what she was thinking—great-grandbabies.

Her eyes twinkled. "Nothing more than friends, huh?"

"So this is how it feels not to be the one in trouble." Courtney smirked. "I kind of like it."

Caleb positioned himself between his family and Becca. "It's not what you think."

"Yes, it is." Grams rubbed her palms together. "And I couldn't be more delighted."

Becca's heart pounded in her chest, a mixture of embarrassment, passion and pride. The way Caleb shielded her from his family like a knight in gray pinstripes made her feel special.

He might be everything she didn't want in a guy, but at this moment she wouldn't want to be with anyone else.

Her lips throbbed. Her breathing wouldn't settle. Her insides ached for more kisses.

She'd experienced those same reactions in Redmond. But something felt different, awakened, as if she'd finally met a man who saw beyond her past and could accept her for who she was today. No guy had ever made her feel like that.

Becca longed to reach forward and lace her fingers with Caleb's in support and solidarity. But that would only fuel Gertie's speculations.

It's not what you think.

But it could be. And the possibility gave Becca hope. Strength. She stepped forward and took her place next to Caleb.

Gertie rose up on her tiptoes, acting more like an excited child than the creative genius of a skin-care empire.

Courtney's snicker turned into a smile, transforming the beautiful young woman from a life-size cardboard cutout of the latest fashion trends to someone more real and genuine.

"People want to see Snowy," Grams said.

Becca glanced back at the dog that stood at his door all fluffed and ready to go. "He's ready."

"We'll bring Snowy up there in a few minutes," Caleb added.

Gertie winked. "Don't take too long."

Her suggestive tone sent heat rushing up Becca's neck.

A vein twitched at Caleb's jaw. "We won't."

Gertie and Courtney, looking as if they were about to burst out laughing, exited the kennel.

As soon as the door shut, Caleb looked down at the ground, shaking his head.

Becca touched his shoulder. "I'm sorry."

His gaze met hers. Softened. "You have nothing to be sorry about."

"But Gertie's going to think—"

Caleb kissed Becca, a gentle whisper of a kiss. The tender brush of his lips made her feel even more cherished, as if she was meant to be treasured. Her chest swelled with affection for this man. He backed away from her slowly, as if he didn't want to end the kiss.

Becca swallowed a sigh. She wished he could keep on kissing her...forever.

"Don't worry about my grandmother or my sister." He touched her face again, lightly tracing her jawline with his thumb. "It doesn't matter what they think is going on between us."

Becca nodded, but she was worried. All they'd done was kiss. But something was happening between her and Caleb, something big. At least, it felt that way to her. If he didn't feel the same...

"I'm happy I finally got to kiss you from beginning to end— even if we were interrupted again. Now that we've finished that, we can go from here."

His words swirled around her and squeezed tight, like a vise grip around her heart. Her breath hitched. Her throat burned.

Caleb wasn't talking about kisses. He wanted more. A hookup. A one-night stand. That was why he'd said what he had to Gertie. The kisses hadn't meant the same thing to him.

Becca's shoulders sagged. At least she'd found out before any real damage had been done. She straightened and raised her chin. "I need to get Snowy."

Caleb's eyes darkened. "What's wrong?"

A "nothing" sat on the tip of her tongue. But "nothing" wouldn't keep her stomach from knotting a thousand different ways. "Nothing" wouldn't keep her from staying up all night analyzing the situation until exhaustion took over.

She'd been there before. She wasn't eager for a return trip.

With a deep breath, she mustered her courage. "So now that we've finished—"

"We—" he twirled a short strand of her hair with his fingertip "—are going on a date."

Hope exploded inside her—short-lived, as caution shouted a warning. "A date?"

"Dinner at Pacifica."

Pacifica was a new restaurant in town. "I've heard Pacifica's incredible, but impossible to get a reservation."

"I'll get us a table."

His confidence attracted her as much as it repelled. Less than a minute ago she was ready to write his kiss and him off. Now she was going on a date with him. The tennis-match-worthy back and forth was enough to make her light-headed.

Becca wasn't interested in his money or power. She liked the way he cared about people and took care of them. But she was pleased he was trying to do something special to make her feel important. She found it endearingly silly because she would be happy going out for hot dogs. "Sounds great."

"Are you free Wednesday?" he asked.

That was only two days away. No worries. He'd never get a table. "I am."

He typed on his smartphone. "This shouldn't take long."

"What are you doing?"

"Making a reservation." His phone buzzed. He stared at the screen. "Wednesday at eight. It's a date."

"How did you manage that?"

"I grew up here." He looked so pleased with himself. "I have a few connections."

And now she had a date with Caleb Fairchild.

The realization of what she'd agreed to hit her like a two-hundred-pound Newfoundland dog wanting a hug. Hope turned to an impending sense of dread. Her sandals felt more like cement blocks. Becca trudged to Snowy.

A date with Caleb Fairchild.

She opened the door and attached Snowy's leash to his collar. She would need something nice to wear, nicer than one of her dog-show suits.

Snowy trotted out.

She would need to know what utensils to use when. Was the saying from the outside in or was it the inside out? She would need to look up rules of etiquette and table manners on the Internet.

She would need to figure out what to say or not say to Gertie about going out with Caleb.

"Snowy looks like a champion," Caleb said.

Becca nodded, but she couldn't relax.

Her muscles bunched. Her stomach clenched.

A date with Caleb Fairchild.

A man who could get a table at the hottest restaurant in town with a simple text was the last guy she should ever want to date. Or kiss. Or…

No falling for him. A date was one thing. A kiss another. Anything more could be…disastrous.

On the patio, Caleb stood back while Gertie, Becca and Snowy took the spotlight. Becca's confidence blossomed around the dog. He wished she exuded the same confidence when she wasn't with one of the dogs.

Courtney sidled up next to him. "Not what you think. Really?"

"Drop it."

"No." She leaned closer, sending a whiff of expensive perfume up his nostrils. "I saw the direction of your hand. Becca didn't seem to mind one bit. You like her."

"I enjoy spending time with her."

"You like her."

Becca stacked Snowy, the way she had in the ring. The dog ate up applause and attention as if it were beef jerky.

"How long have you been dating?" Courtney asked.

"You're not going to let this go."

"You dating someone takes pressure off me."

She flipped her hair behind her shoulder with a practice move rumored to have cut men to their knees. Not any man Caleb would want to know.

"So spill," she said.

"We're not dating, but I'm taking Becca to Pacifica on Wednesday."

"Fancy-schmancy." Courtney used her favorite saying since childhood. The words described his sister's lifestyle perfectly. "You're out to impress Becca."

"I want her to enjoy the evening." But Caleb realized he did want to impress Becca. "I want her to feel comfortable, not intimidated."

Courtney grinned as if she'd been handed a platinum Visa card with no spending limit. "Leave it to me, bro."

Two women couldn't have been more different. He eyed his sister warily. "What do you have in mind?"

Wednesday morning, Becca released the dogs into their run. She cleaned the kennel from top to bottom—sweeping, scrubbing, disinfecting. The entire time she thought about Caleb. Tonight was their date.

She ran through all the things she'd been learning online about eating at an expensive fancy restaurant. Use flatware from the outside in. Napkins are for dabbing, never wiping. Bread should be torn, not cut with a knife. Her parents had taught her a few of the rules like no elbows on the table, don't take a bite until everyone had been served and don't slurp soup or drinks. Maybe she would be able to pull this off.

If not, it was only one date. No big deal.

Yeah, right.

This was the biggest deal since Gertie had hired her.

Mopping the floor outside the dog stalls, Becca pictured the outfit she was going to wear. She'd gone through every piece of clothing she owned and settled on a slim black skirt, white blouse and a pair of black pumps. A scarf would add a burst of color. Silver hoop earrings and a bracelet would be her jewelry.

She wanted to look elegant. Most likely she would be dressed too plainly for a place as trendy and hip as Pacifica.

Maybe she should cancel.

Becca rested against the mop.

You could take a mutt into the show ring, but no matter what she wore or how she acted, the maître d' would know she was a mixed breed, not a purebred. No sense pretending otherwise.

Her cellphone rang. "Hello."

"Please come to the house right now."

The urgency in Gertie's voice made Becca drop the mop. "On my way."

She ran to the house. The family room was empty. The kitchen, too. "Gertie?"

"Upstairs."

Becca climbed the stairs two at a time, her heart racing, worried about Gertie. She entered Gertie's bedroom, her gaze scanning the room. Unique antiques. Luxurious textiles. Exotic treasures.

On the bed was something new. A pile of clothing. Shoes, too.

Gertie stood with a beaming smile on her face and a familiar twinkle in her eyes. Courtney was next to Gertie. Mrs. Harris and Maura were there, too.

"What's going on?" Becca asked.

Courtney motioned to the bed with a pile of clothing and shoes on top. "I have a bunch of stuff that isn't the right color or style. We're about the same size. Maura, too. I thought the two of you might want to see if there's anything you like."

Becca imagined her not unsuitable but not perfect outfit for tonight. She couldn't believe her luck or Courtney's generosity. A lump of gratitude clogged Becca's throat. Tears stung her eyes. She covered her face with her hands.

Gertie put her arm around Becca. "What's wrong, dear?"

"This is so nice. The timing is perfect," Becca sniffled. "I have a date tonight, but I don't have anything nice enough to wear, so I've been thinking about canceling."

"Don't fret," Gertie said in a voice that made it seem as if the world could end and everything would still be okay.

"And please don't cancel," Courtney said. "We'll find you a knockout outfit to wear. Some of the clothes still have the tags on them."

Becca rubbed her eyes. She didn't understand rich people.

"Courtney is a shopaholic. Something she may have inherited from me," Gertie said to Maura and Becca. "It's about time others benefited from my granddaughter's addiction."

Maura stepped forward. "I'd love some new clothes. Tags or not."

Most of Becca's clothes came from thrift stores or consignment shops. She had no issue with hand-me-downs. "Me, too."

"Where are you going tonight?" Gertie asked.

As soon as Becca told them where, they would know she was going with Caleb. But she couldn't lie. "Pacifica."

Both Mrs. Harris and Maura gasped.

A snug smile formed on Courtney's lips.

"A lovely restaurant." Beaming, Gertie led Becca toward the bed. "Let's find something that'll make Caleb's eyes bug out and want to go straight to dessert."

CHAPTER TEN

DINNER AT PACIFICA was a hundred times better than Caleb had expected. It wasn't the mouthwatering Northwest cuisine from the award-winning chef. It wasn't the all-star service from the waiter dressed in black. It wasn't the romantic atmosphere with flickering votive candles and fresh flowers atop a linen-covered table for two. It was the woman sitting across from him who made the night memorable.

Caleb squeezed Becca's hand. "Have I told you how stunning you look tonight?"

Her smile meant only for him made Caleb feel seven feet tall. "About ten times. But I don't mind."

"Then I'll keep saying it." She wore a one-shoulder floral dress with a tantalizing asymmetrical hem. The heels of her strappy sandals accentuated her long legs. She'd glossed her lips and wore makeup. "You're the most beautiful women in Boise."

Her cheeks flushed, a pale pink that made her more attractive. "Only because I had your sister to help me."

"You don't need makeup and clothes to be beautiful." He pointed to her heart. "It's all right there. The rest are optional accessories."

Gratitude shone in the depths of her eyes. "Thank you."

"You're welcome." Caleb didn't have room in his life for a girlfriend. But he liked being with Becca. Maybe she'd be up for a casual relationship. Time permitting. He kissed the top of her hand. "But even though your dress is spectacular, I kind of miss seeing you covered in dog hair."

Her laughter, as melodic as a song, caressed his heart.

"I doubt they would have let me in with a speck of hair or lint on me." She glanced around, then lowered her voice. "I'm so relieved I made it through dinner. I kept thinking if I made a mistake, used the wrong fork or something, they'd kick me out."

"You didn't make any mistakes."

She kissed his hand. "It wasn't as hard as I thought it would be."

Their waiter, dressed in a black tuxedo with a gleaming bald head and an equally bright smile, dropped off the leather case containing Caleb's credit card and the bill.

Becca rubbed his hand with her thumb. "Thank you for tonight. I'll never forget this evening."

He wouldn't, either. "We'll have to do it again."

"I'd like that, but…"

"What?"

Mischief filled her eyes. "You've given me a peek into your world. If we do this again, I want to show you mine."

"Not if, when. That sounds like fun."

She shimmied her shoulders, as if excited.

Caleb wanted to lean across the table and kiss her bare shoulder, then trail more kisses up her neck until he reached her lips.

"How does Friday sound?" he asked.

"This Friday?"

He might not want a girlfriend, but a few dates didn't mean anything. He liked hanging out with Becca. No big deal. He could walk away any time. But for now he would enjoy her. "Yes."

On Thursday, Becca printed out a stack of emails for Gertie. "These are product orders. Too bad we don't have any products to sell."

Gertie's smile kept widening as she thumbed through the pages. "We can make up some batches in the lab. Sell those."

"Is that legal?"

"We're using natural, known ingredients, so we shouldn't have a problem." Gertie looked at Becca. "But double-check with Caleb to be on the safe side."

Becca would love to hear his voice. His good-night kiss in the parking lot had tempted her, but common sense won out over raging hormones. She was growing fonder of him each time she saw him. Still no sense taking a swan dive into an empty pool. "I'll text him."

She didn't really need to hear his voice.

Gertie tapped her chin. "We should pick a show, set up a booth and debut the products."

"Stumptown is in July, but that's too soon. The Enumclaw show is a couple weeks later in August. That one draws people from all over and has lots of breed specialties going on, too."

"Sounds good. Mark your calendar."

August wasn't that far way. "It's going to be a busy summer with all the dog shows we've entered."

"Have Caleb go with you."

Thinking about spending the summer at dog shows with Caleb made her pulse race faster than a Greyhound chasing a rabbit. But Becca could never ask him to do that. She couldn't lower her guard that much and open herself up to more heartache. "We're not…"

"Friends? I've seen the way he looks at you." Gertie raised a white eyebrow. "He's never looked at another woman like that. Not even his ex-fiancée."

Becca had heard about his ex from Courtney the other night doing Becca's makeup for her date. Becca realized how much Caleb and she had in common with their past romances. No wonder he hadn't trusted her when he first met her. It would be hard to trust anyone after almost being scammed by someone who claimed to love you. At least they were past that now.

"That makes you happy." Gertie said.

Yes, very much so. But Becca didn't dare admit that aloud.

A little voice inside her head whispered a warning. The caution reverberated through her. Getting her hopes up too high could mean a long, hurtful drop. The last thing she wanted—needed—was for her heart to go splat. But there was something she could say. "Caleb is a nice guy."

"Yes, but my grandson is still a man," Gertie said. "They'll take whatever you offer and try to keep the status quo as long as possible."

"I don't understand."

"Don't sleep with Caleb until there's a wedding band on your finger."

Becca's cheeks burned. "We've only kissed a few times."

"Some pretty hot kisses from what I saw."

She covered her mouth with her hand, unable to believe Gertie talked so openly about kissing and…sex.

"Don't be embarrassed. I might be old, but I was young once," Gertie said. "Remember the adage about the cow and getting milk for free is as true today as it was when I was your age."

Becca knew her boss had only her best interest at heart, but this was awkward. "I'll remember."

Not that she and Caleb were even close to…that. Taking things to the next level would be a game changer.

What had Caleb said?

Win-win.

She'd always come out on the losing side before. She didn't see that changing, even if a part of her wished it would.

But Becca knew one thing. She wasn't sure she was ready to trust her heart again. Or if she ever could.

Friday evening, Caleb arrived at what looked to be an Old West saloon for his date with Becca. He hadn't seen her in two days, two of the longest days of his life.

If he wasn't thinking about her, he was texting her. If he wasn't texting her, he was figuring out the best time to call her.

If he wasn't calling her, he was back to thinking about her. A vicious cycle. One that left him distracted and behind at work. One he wasn't used to and wanted to stop.

No matter. This wasn't some serious relationship. They shared a few interests and sizzling chemistry. That was what drew him to her, nothing more.

Becca stood outside the restaurant, waiting for him. She wore jean shorts, a red lace-trimmed camisole with a red gingham button-down shirt over it.

His heart tripped over itself at the sight of her. His temperature skyrocketed at the tan, toned skin showing.

"You came straight from the office," she said.

"I got stuck in a meeting." He kissed her cheek. She smelled sweet like strawberries. "I'm overdressed."

"Take off your jacket and tie."

"It's fine."

She tugged on his tie. "I'm serious. You need to take this off now."

"Don't worry."

"You're going to regret not—"

He touched his finger to his lips. "Shhh."

"Your loss."

Caleb had no idea what she was talking about. "How was your day?"

"Good. I reviewed our new website and made a list of changes for the web designer."

"Text me the URL. I can't wait to see it."

"Courtney came up with the name. Gertie's Top Dog Products."

He opened the door to the restaurant. "I'm surprised Grams dragged my sister into this."

Becca entered. "Courtney wanted to help."

"She must have an ulterior motive."

"Being nice isn't enough?"

"Not for my sister." Inside, he took a step. Something

crunched beneath his shoe. He looked down. Peanut shells. "Interesting floor covering."

The entire place was interesting. The hole-in-the-wall grill was a far cry from Pacifica. The smell of hops and grease filled the air. The din of customer's conversations and cussing rose above the honky-tonk music playing from speakers.

Becca pointed to a No Ties sign. "You should take yours off."

"No one cares what I wear here."

She dragged two fingers over her mouth, zipping her lips. "Won't mention it again."

The hostess wore supertight, short jean shorts, a spaghetti-strap top and a ponytail. She led them to a table.

Caleb sat across from Becca. A tin pail full of shelled peanuts sat in the center of the table next to a roll of paper towels.

The hostess handed them menus. "Your server will be right with you."

He looked around. Customers had engraved their names on the wood planks covering the walls. He doubted they used a butter knife. That told him a lot about the clientele. He would have to bring Ty here the next time his friend was home. "Come here often?"

"No, but it's one of my favorite places in town."

"I've never heard of it."

"It's time you discovered one of Boise's hidden gems."

Hidden, yes. A gem? Becca would have to convince Caleb. But he had no doubt Ty would love this place.

Caleb read the menu. Lots of red meat and potatoes. Fried, French, mashed, baked. Okay, maybe this place was okay.

"Howdy, partners. I'm Jackie, your server." A perky, voluptuous woman with equally puffy big hair stood at their table. She wore tight jean shorts and a T-shirt two sizes too small. "I see we have a new visitor to our fine establishment. Welcome, fine sir. I take it you did not see the sign."

"What sign?"

Becca shook her head.

"The No Ties sign," Jackie said.

"I saw it," he admitted.

"Then there's only one thing left for me to do." She pulled out a pair of scissors from her back pocket, leaned toward him giving him a bird's-eye view of her breasts and cut off his tie right above one side of the knot.

"What the…" He stared at where his tie used to hang. The spot was empty. "That was a silk tie."

An expensive one.

"I told you," Becca said. "More than once, if you remember."

"You never said they'd vandalize my tie."

Jackie shrugged. "You saw the sign. You disobeyed the sign. You pay the price."

This was unbelievable. "What happens to the tie now?"

"It becomes part of our decor," Jackie said. "Look up."

Caleb did. Hundreds of colorful ties hung from the ceiling.

"You should have listened to me," Becca said. "But I didn't try that hard to convince you. I've never been all that fond of your yellow tie. No big loss, if you want my opinion."

"Red is a power color." Jackie tucked the tie into her bra. A good thing they had a use for it, because he wasn't going to want it back now. "Yellow is too…"

"Understated," Becca said.

Unbelievable. His grandmother had said the same things. He half laughed.

"You've got your peanuts and menus and sense of humor," Jackie said. "I'll be back in a jiff to take your drink orders."

With that, the server walked away.

"I hope you're not too upset about your tie?" Becca asked.

"Not upset," he admitted. "It's my fault. You warned me. I chose not to listen to you. Lesson learned."

With a smile, Becca grabbed a handful of peanuts. "Dig in."

He took one from the pail. "You just toss the shells on the floor?"

"You've led a sheltered life. Watch." She illustrated what to do. "Your turn."

Caleb took another peanut. Opened it. Removed the peanut. Tossed the shell on the ground.

"Easy-peasy." She dumped a handful of peanuts in front of him, then pointed to a target painted on the aisle between the tables. "Now we can get serious. High point wins."

That sounded fun. "What's the prize?"

She shrugged. "What do you want it to be?"

You. In the horizontal position. But he didn't think she was up for that. At least not yet. Maybe later tonight. "I don't care."

"Then I'll have to think of something—until then…go for it."

With each peanut shell he tossed, the stress of his day spent working at Fair Face and attending meetings slipped away. Nothing mattered, not Grams or Courtney. There was only here and now. And Becca.

He threw another peanut. "This is more fun than I thought it would be."

"Fun is the name of the game here."

Caleb saw that. He liked it, too. "I like having fun."

Becca had brought fun back into his life. The kind of fun Grams said he needed. And Caleb knew one thing.

He didn't want it to end.

At least not anytime soon.

Becca didn't want the night to end. Delicious food. Interesting conversation. A handsome date who made her think of slow, hot kisses.

Charmed by Caleb, yes. Totally enchanted by him—she was on her way.

Time to pull back. Though that was hard to do when he held her hand in the restaurant's parking lot.

"I had a great time tonight," Caleb said. "Want to get together tomorrow and go tie shopping?"

Her heart leaped. Common sense frowned. She laughed, not knowing if he were serious or not.

"I mean it."

Okay, he was serious. She bit her lip.

The list of reasons she shouldn't want to see him again was long. But those things were easy to forget when Caleb's gaze made her feel like the only woman in the world. His world, at least. That could be oh-so-dangerous. "You should ask your sister to go. I know nothing about ties."

He brushed his lips over Becca's hair, making her knees want to melt. "Courtney might know fashion, but you know me."

Her heart bumped. The thought of spending more time with Caleb made her want to cancel her plans. But she couldn't. "I would love to go tie shopping, but I'm driving down to see my parents tomorrow."

"Overnight?"

"A day trip," she said. "I need to be back for the dogs."

"Ah, yes, the dogs."

He sounded funny. "What do you mean by the dogs?"

"I never thought I'd be jealous of some pups."

"Jealous, huh?"

"You're at their beck and call."

"It's my job."

"Admit it," he said lightheartedly. "You like the dogs better than you like me."

He was teasing, but there was some truth to his words. Becca liked dogs better than most people. But better than Caleb?

"It's a different kind of like," she said. "Dogs are loyal, protective and think I'm the center of their universe. That's pretty appealing."

"True, but a dog can't do this."

Caleb dipped his head, touching his mouth to Becca's. Electric. His lips moved over hers, sending pleasurable tingles shooting through her. She savored the feel and the taste of him. Forget the dinner they'd eaten, this was all she needed for nourishment. He drew the kiss to an end much to soon.

"You're right." She rubbed her throbbing lips together. "A dog can't to that."

His chest expanded. "Damn straight they can't."

She laughed. "Thanks for dinner. It's been a lovely evening."

"We don't have to call it a night."

Oh, Becca was tempted. But keeping her heart under lock and key was becoming more difficult each time they were together.

Thanks to Caleb, she felt more confident, competent, sexy. She liked it. Liked him. And felt herself growing closer to him. But she wasn't sure she could trust her feelings. Or his. He didn't seem eager to get into a relationship. She had avoided them herself. "There's no reason to rush into anything, right?"

"No," he said. "But I would like to see you tomorrow. How about I go with you to your parents' house?"

She stared at him in disbelief. "Seriously?"

He nodded. "You know Grams. Seems fair I should meet your parents."

"Sure." Becca wiggled her toes. "That would be great."

On Saturday afternoon, Caleb drove into the trailer park outside Twin Falls. He wasn't sure what to expect, but so far seemed stereotypical. Singlewides, doublewides and RVs filled the various lots. Cars and trucks were parked haphazardly on the narrow streets. Cats lounged in the sun. Dogs barked at his car.

"Turn left at the Statue of Liberty. You can't miss it," Becca said.

"I'm looking forward to meeting your parents."

"They can't wait to meet you."

A six-foot replica of the Statue of Liberty stood like a sentry at an intersection. Nearby, two men with handlebar mustaches and tattooed arms eyed his sports car. An elderly woman sat in a rocking chair with a Chihuahua on her lap on the porch of another trailer.

Becca pointed out the windshield. "My parents live in the trailer with the chicken wire fencing and the Jolly Roger flag."

O-kay. Caleb gripped his steering wheel and parked. Not only was there chicken fencing, but also live chickens. Was that even legal in the city limits? He turned off the ignition.

"My parents are normal folks, so don't be nervous," she said.

A couple thoughts ran through his mind. One, this was going to be interesting, if not enlightening. Two, he doubted he'd ever see the hubcaps on his car again. At least he had insurance. "I'm not nervous."

Not much anyway.

"Good, because I am."

Caleb fought the urge to kiss her nerves away. He squeezed her hand. "No reason to be nervous. They're your parents."

"Exactly." She rewarded him with a grin. "If my father wants to show you his gun and knife collection, say no. Otherwise, he'll try to intimidate you."

Caleb knew from what Becca had told him as well as the private investigator's report that her father had been arrested and jailed for fighting, so this didn't surprise him. "Good to know."

"If my mom mentions UFOs and government conspiracies, smile and nod. Whatever you do, don't mention Roswell or Flight 800."

"Maybe I should have brought a tinfoil hat."

"If you had, you would endear yourself to her forever." Becca moistened her lips. "I'm not kidding."

Her serious tone told him she wasn't.

If Becca considered this "normal folks," he wondered what her version of not-so-normal would be like. Given the Taylors' daughter had grown up to be such a lovely, caring and hardworking woman, he shouldn't rush to judgment. He'd made that mistake with Becca. "Let's go meet your folks."

A man and a woman in their early forties stood on the porch and waved.

"That's my mom and dad, Debbie and Rob," Becca said.

The woman had the same brown hair as Becca, only longer,

and a similar smile. The man had lighter brown hair and the same blue eyes as his daughter. "They look so young."

More like an older brother and sister, not her parents.

"My mom was seventeen and my dad eighteen when they got married. I arrived a week before her eighteenth birthday."

"Kids having kids."

"They thought they were grown up enough at the time, but both told me I should wait until I was older, maybe even in my thirties, to get married."

He opened the gate for Becca. "Good advice."

"Make sure none of the chickens escape."

Caleb closed the gate behind him and double-checked the latch was secure.

Introductions were made. Becca's parents were friendly. He received a handshake from Rob and a hug from Debbie. The four of them entered the house. Their trailer was small, tidy and welcoming. Pictures hung on the walls. Knick-knacks covered shelves. But no pets. Not a dog or a cat in sight. That surprised him given Becca's love of animals.

Caleb studied the photographs of a young Becca riding a tricycle and one of her winning a ribbon at a 4-H dog show.

He motioned to her high school graduation picture. "You used to have long hair like your mom's."

She nodded. "I'm not that same person anymore. I like my hair shorter."

"I like it, too," Caleb said, noticing her parents watching the exchange with interest.

"Why don't you help your mother with dinner," Rob said to Becca. "I'll keep Caleb company."

Becca followed Debbie into the kitchen.

Rob slapped him on the back. "So Caleb, you into guns and hunting?"

He remembered what Becca had told him, but he wasn't about to be intimidated. "My grandfather used to take my best friend and me elk hunting. Crossbows, not guns."

"Bag anything?"

"A buck." Caleb remembered his surprise when he'd hit the animal. He'd felt a burst of excitement at making the shot and a rush of sadness at seeing the elk fall. "He was so much bigger than me. Had a helluva time getting him back to camp."

Bob looked toward the kitchen. "I've done some bear hunting."

Caleb expected to be invited to see the gun collection next.

Bob leaned closer. "Never could bring anything I shot home or Becca would cry. You might not want to mention that elk. She's fond of animals. Might hold it against you."

So much for being intimidated. "Thanks for the advice."

"You're welcome." Bob's gaze drifted to the kitchen again. He lowered his voice. "My daughter's caught some bad breaks."

"Becca told me."

"She works hard. Sends us money, even when she doesn't have much herself." Rob's gaze met Caleb's in understanding. "I don't want to see my little girl hurt."

"Me, either. She's a special woman."

"Good to hear you say that," Rob said. "Becca's never brought a man, or a boy for that matter, home before."

Caleb straightened. That surprised him. But she hadn't asked him home to meet her parents. He'd invited himself. She must be taking her parents' advice about waiting to get married until she was older. She had goals and dreams. The last thing she needed was a boyfriend to get in the way. The same way he didn't need a girlfriend. This would make life easier for both of them.

They wouldn't have to worry about things getting serious and complicated. They could keep having fun together and enjoying each other's company.

Yes, this was going to work out well.

In the kitchen, Becca put the tray of biscuits into the preheated oven. She set the timer. "Dinner smells good."

"Meatloaf with mashed potatoes and pie for dessert," her mother said. "Caleb's handsome."

"He's got the prettiest eyes and the nicest smile."

"You really like him."

"We haven't been seeing each other long."

"That doesn't mean you can't have feelings for him." Her mother stirred the gravy simmering on the stove. "I knew your father was the one a week after we met."

Becca had heard the story of how they met at a local burger joint over chocolate milk shakes and French fries many times. "How did you know?"

"It was a feeling." Her mother tilted her head. "We fit from that very first day. When we were apart it wasn't awful like the world was ending or someone had died, but when we were to-gether things were better. We were a team. We complemented each other. If that makes sense."

That was how Becca felt with Caleb. "It does."

"Do you think you and Caleb might turn into something serious?"

Yes! She was afraid to voice her desire aloud. Afraid to be-lieve in a happily ever after with him. "Maybe."

Her mother removed a bottle of salad dressing from the re-frigerator. "How does he make you feel?"

"Special. Important. Like I can do anything." Her breath caught. "I think I'm falling for him."

"You think?"

Becca laughed. "Okay, I'm falling. I may have already fallen. It feels scary."

"Falling for someone is very scary. That's a normal feeling. But good, too." Her mother touched her shoulder. "You can't live stuck in the past. Afraid. Caleb isn't Whitley. If you like Caleb, give him a chance."

"I always thought all I needed in my life were dogs, but after meeting Caleb…"

Kissing him…

"You want more," her mom said.

"Yes." Becca not only wanted more, she needed more. That terrified her. The last time she wanted more, she'd ended up heartbroken and in jail. She hated to think that could happen with Caleb, too. "But we're so different. I'm not sure it can work. Do you think I can really fit into Caleb's world?"

"Yes. Just be yourself. If who you are doesn't fit, then he's not the right man for you."

"Mom."

"I'm serious." Her mother wrapped her arms around Becca. "You are a sweet, generous, smart woman with so much love to give the right man."

"I think Caleb might be the right man for me."

"Only time will tell."

Caleb wouldn't waste hours to drive to her parents' house if she didn't mean something to him. He acted as if he accepted her and her past. He called, texted and wanted to spend time with her. He had feelings for her. The only question was what kind of feelings. "I hope it doesn't take long."

"Patience is a virtue," her mother said.

Becca checked the biscuits. "I spent three years being patient. You'd think I'd get a break this time."

"Sorry to say, baby, but there aren't many breaks when it comes to love."

Love.

Becca liked the sound of that, liked it a lot.

She only hoped Caleb would, too.

And this time wouldn't turn out to be another big mistake.

CHAPTER ELEVEN

FOUR HOURS LATER, the headlights of Caleb's car cut through the darkness. Becca sat in the passenger seat, cocooned in the comfy, leather seats. Looking at his handsome profile, warmth flowed through her. "I thought the visit went well."

He glanced her way. "I had fun. Your parents are great."

"They like you."

"I like them." Caleb maneuvered the car around an orange semi-truck. "Your dad didn't pull out any guns or knives."

"Lucky," she teased. "He'd threatened to do that if you turned out to be a bozo or an idiot."

"Good to know I'm neither of those things." He readjusted his hands on the steering wheel. "Your mom is a kick. She should have been a lawyer. She had me almost convinced we never landed on the moon."

Becca laughed. "My mom can argue with the best of them."

"But I'm glad she had you instead of going on to college."

The pitter-patter of her heart tripled. "Me, too."

"What's your week like?" he asked.

"Busy. There's a local dog show on Saturday and Sunday. I'm going to be driving back and forth each day. We're too busy producing products in the lab for me to be away."

"It's going to be a busy week for me, too."

Bummer, but she wasn't about to complain after spending today with him. "Maybe we can see each other online."

"We'll figure something out."

The perfect end to a perfect day. Well that, and Caleb's toe-curling good-night kiss.

After he left, Becca brought the dogs to the guest cottage. "I'm in such a good mood you guys can sleep with me tonight."

She changed into a pair of flannel shorts and T-shirt and closed the blinds.

With two dogs on the bed with her, another three on the floor and a laptop in front of her, she answered emails about the products, a result of the samples she'd been handing out at dog shows and word of mouth. The lab had been turned into a mini-manufacturing plant, but Gertie's research assistants were taking the temporary change in job responsibilities in stride.

Becca's cellphone rang.

She glanced at the clock on the nightstand—11:28 p.m. Late for a call. Unless it was Caleb.

Adrenaline surged. She grabbed the phone. The name on the screen read Courtney Fairchild.

Becca hit answer. "Courtney?"

"Sorry to call so late." Courtney sniffled. "I'm in a bit of a jam."

The words came out stilted. Something was wrong. "What's going on?"

"My, um, car's in the Boise River."

Concern ricocheted through Becca. "Are you hurt?"

Her sharp voice woke the dogs. Maurice tried to climb on her lap. Hunter jumped off the bed.

"I'm…I think I'm okay." Courtney's voice quivered. "My car is ruined. Caleb's going to kill me. That's why I called you and not him or Grams. You won't be mad at me."

"Of course I'm not mad." Becca changed out of her pajamas and into clothes. "Where are you?"

Courtney gave her the crossroads. "Just follow the flashing lights. I'm going to need a ride home. If I don't end up going to the hospital. There's a cute firefighter who thinks I should go."

"Listen to him."

"Okay. I'll do whatever he says." Courtney sounded strange,

mixed up, in shock. "I can't believe I ruined another car. Caleb's going to…"

"Don't worry about your brother." Becca slipped on her sandals. "I'm going to put the dogs in the kennel, then drive over. If you're not at the river, I'll drive to the nearest hospital, okay?"

"Thanks. I appreciate this."

Becca hoped Caleb wouldn't be upset for not calling him immediately. But she'd been in a similar spot. Calling anyone was difficult. She was happy to be there for Courtney, and as soon as Becca knew more she'd contact Caleb. "See you soon."

Hours later, Becca dozed in the waiting room of the hospital. She'd been sitting with Courtney until they took her for more tests due to the nasty bump on her head.

"What are you doing here?"

She opened her eyes to see a not-so-happy-looking Caleb standing in front of her. His gaze was narrowed. His mouth set in a firm, thin line. No wonder Courtney didn't want to call him.

"Courtney called me. She was hurting," Becca said. "Scared."

"My sister should be terrified." He shifted his weight from foot to foot. "Texting while driving. She could have been killed or killed somebody else."

"Thankfully, she wasn't, and she didn't."

"Her car is ruined."

"The airbag saved her life."

Caleb looked tense like a spring ready to pop open. His jaw was as rigid as a steel girder.

Becca touched his arm. His muscles bunched beneath her palm. "Courtney's going to be okay."

"This time. Like the last time." He exhaled slowly. "One of these times she won't be. That will kill Grams."

And him.

Becca could tell this was tearing Caleb up inside. She put her arm around him.

His body stiffened tightly—she might as well be hugging

a tree. He backed out of her embrace. "You shouldn't butt into my family's business."

Where had that come from? He was upset. She realized that, but his words were like a slap to her cheek. She took a breath. And another. "I'm not butting in. I told you Courtney called me."

Suspicion filled his gaze. Something she hadn't seen since they first met. "Why didn't you call me?"

"Courtney wasn't ready to see you."

"And you didn't think I should know what happened to my sister."

Becca tried not to take his anger personal. "It was late. If her injuries had been more serious—"

"The police thought it was serious enough to call me."

"The police?"

"I'm co-owner of the car. But that's the last time I do that." He brushed his hand through his hair. "Courtney needs to deal with the consequences of her actions. Clean up her messes. Not have others do it for her."

"She's still young."

"Only a year younger than you."

That surprised Becca. "She seems younger."

"That's because Courtney still acts like a spoiled little girl. She's too much like our father. My grandmother bailed him out of so many jams he never learned from his mistakes. Courtney's the same way."

"Learning from mistakes isn't always easy," Becca said. "Sometimes the lessons are so in your face it's hard to miss them. But other times it's not as clear."

He studied her for a moment, the anger clearing from his eyes. "You learned."

"I had three years to think about what I did."

But right now she wondered if she'd learned anything during that time. One thing was clear tonight. Caleb didn't want her here. He wanted to keep family stuff private. She ignored the sting in her heart. She needed to focus on Courtney right now.

Becca took a deep breath. "The point is everyone makes mistakes."

Including Caleb.

"Courtney makes more mistakes than most."

"You're her big brother." Becca softened her tone. If only he could see that he was making a big mistake with his younger sister. "Help Courtney figure out what she should be doing instead of getting into so much trouble."

"I've tried."

The anguish in his voice hurt Becca's heart. She touched his back. This time he didn't tense. "Try harder. You have a lot on your plate, but Courtney is your sister. I just met her, but it's clear she's bored out of her mind. She hates her job at Fair Face."

"She's never in the office."

"Why not?"

"She's off shopping or sleeping in late."

"So Gertie isn't the only one who lets Courtney get away with stuff."

"My sister is a handful."

"Yes, but threatening to kill her or cut her off from her trust fund if she messes up isn't helping matters."

"I don't want her to end up like our dad."

"No one does, but she's not happy. You can't force her to work at a job she doesn't want. She might be better off working in a different department or even another company," Becca said. "Getting Courtney pointed in the right direction isn't enabling her. It's supporting her. Helping her. That's what family does for one another."

"I'm being a jerk."

"Courtney will understand."

"I meant with you." He touched Becca's face. His gaze softened. "I wasn't expecting to see you here. It caught me off-guard."

"I understand."

And Becca did. She might want to let Caleb into her life

and heart, but he wasn't there yet. For all she knew, he might never be there.

And that realization sucked.

The week dragged for Caleb. He hadn't seen Becca since the night at the hospital. He'd been a jerk to her. But he couldn't help himself.

Grams adored Becca. Courtney turned to Becca in her time of need. Caleb wanted to spend all his free time with Becca.

She'd become a pivotal person in his family. Something no one, not even Cassandra, had managed to do.

That bothered him. Immensely.

She'd gotten under his skin, but he couldn't allow her into his heart. He wasn't ready to get into something too deep. Not that she was pushing him into a relationship. Or had mentioned the word.

Maybe all he needed was distance.

So he didn't call her the rest of the week. Didn't text her.

But that didn't stop him from thinking about her.

He'd tried focusing on work, but thinking about her interfered with him accomplishing much. Sitting through one boring meeting after another hadn't taken his mind off her.

And here he was again in another meeting on a Friday afternoon.

To make matters worse, there was a weird vibe in the conference room. He looked around the table, pen between his fingers.

Glen, the vice president of Sales and Marketing, checked his watch for the twelfth time in the past fifteen minutes. Ed, the usually messy director of advertising, played housekeeper—wiping off the table, pushing in unused chairs and straightening papers. Julie, the new head of PR, kept sneaking peeks at the door as if HGTV were about to burst in and award her a dream house.

People were ready to kick off their weekends, but that didn't explain why the three of them were acting so strange.

Caleb tapped his pen against the table. "Anything else we need to discuss?"

Glances passed between them. Glen to Ed. Ed to Julie. Julie to Glen. All over Caleb's head. They might as well have been tossing a ball back and forth for their lack of subtlety.

"What's going on?" Caleb asked.

"Nothing."

"Nada."

"Not a thing."

The three spoke at the same time, their words falling on top of each other.

Something was definitely going on. He might be the CEO, the closest thing to a puppet master Fair Face had, but right now he felt as if someone else was manipulating the strings. He didn't like it.

"Talk to me," he said, using his hard-as-nails-don't-mess-with-me CEO voice he'd perfected for use in conference calls with suppliers.

Another shared glance passed among the three.

Glen cleared his throat. "Just a little anxious."

Caleb understood wanting to go home. He hadn't made plans to see Becca tonight, but maybe it wasn't too late. "Let's call it, then."

Julie jumped to her feet, her brown eyes widening and her gaze darting to the door. "Wait!"

Both Glen and Ed nodded furiously like Buster Bronco–the Boise State mascot—bobble-head dolls.

"I thought you wanted to get out of here," Caleb said.

"There's one more thing." Julie practically skipped away from the table, her shoulder-length red hair swinging behind her. She opened the door.

A bright light shone into the conference room.

Caleb dropped his pen. "What's—"

An attractive woman dressed in a maroon suit burst into the room. She held a microphone in one hand and a bottle of champagne in the other. Her straight, bleached teeth were as blinding as the camera light behind her.

"I'm Savannah Martin with *Good Day Boise*." The woman pronounced each word with precision. "Congratulations, Caleb Fairchild, you've been named Boise's Bachelor of the Year."

What the…

With lightning-quick moves that would make a ninja in high heels proud, Savannah thrust the champagne into his hands and shoved the microphone into his face. "Exciting news, isn't it?"

Caleb's gut churned, as if the gyro he'd eaten for lunch was waging war on his internal organs. He had no idea what being Bachelor of the Year entailed, but he doubted any of the hoopla would include Becca.

A predatory gleam filled the reporter's eyes, making him think she'd eat her young to get a story.

Not having a clue what to say, he stood. After all, that was the polite thing to do. Sweat dampened the back of his neck under his lightly starched collar. "Thank you."

The words rushed out faster than he'd intended. But he hadn't planned on being ambushed by the media and his own people.

Where was Ty when Caleb needed him? No one had his six here.

He glanced at the champagne and composed himself with a breath. "This is quite…an honor."

"Indeed." Savannah batted her eyelashes. Predator or flirt? "You had several nominations."

Who would have nominated him for Bachelor of the Year?

Not Grams's style, but Caleb wouldn't put it past Courtney with her odd sense of humor.

Caleb now knew why his coworkers had been acting so strangely during the meeting. The three stood together grinning like fools, as if year-end bonuses were going to arrive five months early. No doubt they'd had a hand in a few of the nominations. But…why?

"This is unexpected." He wished they had picked some

other bachelor in town, someone who cared about this sort of thing. "I'm...stunned."

"I'm not." Savannah gave him a look that would make Jack Frost blush. "Trust me, ladies, this is one bachelor you most definitely want to get to know better. He's a hot one."

Hot, yes. Because of the damn light in his face.

Caleb didn't know how to respond, so he kept smiling instead, a tight smile that hurt the muscles all the way to his toes.

The reporter failed to sense his discomfort or his plastic smile. She seemed more interested in the camera than in him. "This is Savannah Martin with Fair Face CEO, Caleb Fairchild, Boise's Bachelor of the Year."

The light went off. The camera lowered.

He could see again. And breathe. But that didn't loosen the bunched muscles in his shoulders or the fist-sized knot in his stomach.

A twentysomething man with a goatee and wearing faded jeans with a green T-shirt walked out of the meeting room carrying the camera.

Savannah's smile dimmed, as if her on switch connected to the camera's power button. "See you on Tuesday."

"Tuesday?" Caleb asked. Did he look as dazed as he felt?

"At the studio." The reporter's gaze ran the length of him—slow, methodical, appreciative.

She needed to stop looking at him like that. Becca wouldn't like it.

Whoa. Shock reverberated through him. He'd never worried about other women sizing him up when he was engaged to Cassandra. He shouldn't care now. Becca didn't own him. They weren't serious or exclusive. Had he gotten in deeper than he realized?

Julie skipped forward still looking as if she was in a hazy, dreamy mode. "You're being interviewed by *Good Day Boise*. I have all the details."

This was totally insane. There'd better be a good reason for the insanity, or three people would be looking for new jobs come Monday.

"See you on Tuesday, then." Caleb tried to keep his voice pleasant. Savannah left the room, closing the door behind her. "Sit."

His three employees took their places. Caleb sat, placed the champagne bottle on the table and let his smile drop. "What the hell was that all about?"

Ed and Julie looked at Glen, who twirled his pen like a baton. The pen rotated faster and faster.

Caleb's annoyance increased at the same rate of spin. He shot his vice president a tell-me-now-if-you-know-what's-good-for-you look. "Glen."

"My wife told me about the contest," he said. "I thought it would be good publicity for Fair Face."

"I agreed," Ed said.

"Me, too," Julie added. "It's a fantastic opportunity."

"Boise's Bachelor of the Year?" The words tasted bitter in Caleb's mouth. He picked up his pen and tapped it against the table. "Sure about this?"

Because he wasn't.

Two months ago, he would have popped open the champagne to celebrate. Two months ago, he would have phoned his grandmother to share the news. Two months ago, he would have texted Ty to rub it in.

Two months ago, Caleb hadn't known Becca Taylor.

He couldn't stop thinking about her melodic laughter and her hot kisses and when he could see her.

Even if seeing her again didn't make sense.

He didn't know what to think. Do. Say.

"This is a no brainer," Ed said. "Rave reviews about the baby line products are pouring in. Mothers are calling asking for samples. This is perfect timing."

"You can't buy this kind of PR," Glen said. "That's why we nominated you."

"The three of you?" Caleb asked.

"Our staffs," Glen admitted.

"And a few other employees." Ed made it sound like no big deal, but for all Caleb knew the entire company had nominated him. "This is a win-win situation for everyone involved."

It was lose-lose for him. Someone—okay, Becca—would be upset. That would make him unhappy.

Ed rested his elbows on the table. "We need you to play this right to maximize our exposure."

It sounded so calculated. Business often was, especially with advertising, and Caleb's job was to be the perfect CEO and present the correct image to the public. His grandfather had instilled that into him. "Tell me the slant."

Julie opened a manila folder. "Play up being single, but how you're looking to settle down."

Caleb drew back. "Whoa. Settle down?"

"And have a family," Julie said.

His empty hand slapped the table. The harsh sound echoed in the room. "What?"

"Mentioning you want a family will be the perfect segue to Fair Face's new baby products. The whole reason Gertie created the line is because she wants great-grandchildren, right?"

Caleb shifted in his chair. "Ri-i-i-ight."

"But you don't want to mention Gertie. This is about you, not your grandmother." The strategic glint in Glen's eye made him look more like a shark wearing a tie than a business executive. "Say you can't wait to use the new organic, all-natural baby products on your kids."

Caleb imagined Becca, her stomach round with their child. What the hell? He shook the image from his head. "I'm not married. Having kids is years off."

Julie's excited eyes and flushed face made her look as if she were about to bounce out of her chair. "That's where the contest comes in."

Ed nodded. "*Good Day Boise* wants to run a contest on their website."

"What's the prize?" Caleb asked.

Glen smiled. "A date with you."

Caleb stared in disbelief. "Please tell me you're kidding."

"This isn't any old date," Julie said, as if he hadn't said a word. "A dream date. Limousine. Romantic dinner for two at Pacifica. A dance club."

That was where he'd taken Becca on their first date. He couldn't take another woman—make that the contest winner—there.

"You can also do whatever else you want once the official date is over," Glen said with a wink-wink, nudge-nudge to his voice.

Caleb slunk in his chair. Becca was not going to like this.

Not that she had a claim on him, but just the fact he was putting her feeling first was out of character for him. He didn't understand it. He wanted it to stop.

"We'll do a billboard to promote the contest somewhere visible where most of Boise can see," Ed said. "We'll put it on the Facebook page. Take it national if we can. Offer a plane ticket and hotel accommodations if the winner isn't from Boise."

"Who picks the winner?" Caleb asked.

Julie rubbed her palms together as if she were trying to spark a fire. "A modern-day matchmaker."

Dream dates. Matchmaker. "This has to be a joke."

"Do I look like I'm joking?" Glen looked ultra-serious, as if the fate of the company were riding on this. "Your qualities for the perfect woman will be listed on *Good Day Boise*'s website. Viewers who believe they qualify can fill out a profile and see if they're a match."

He tossed his pen. It skidded across the table. "That's…"

"Marketing genius," Ed said. "If you end up dating the winner—"

"Imagine if you marry her," Julie said, her voice rising with each word as if Caleb was such a grand prize.

His stomach roiled. He was going to be sick. And it had nothing to do with what he'd eaten for lunch.

He needed to speak up, put an end to the craziness. "I'm seeing someone."

"Seeing?" Glen asked. "Or dating?"

Caleb hesitated. "It's not that serious."

It wasn't. So why was Becca branded on his brain? Affecting his working life? His family? Why was he putting her feelings ahead of what was best for Fair Face?

"Then it shouldn't be a problem," Glen said.

Caleb wished he had that much confidence. He didn't want to hurt Becca's feelings. They might not be that serious, but he didn't want to do anything to push her away. At least not that far away. "Put yourself in my shoes."

"A pair or two of new shoes might soothe any hurt feelings," Julie suggested.

Becca couldn't care less about fancy shoes. But she might like a new pair of grooming scissors. So not enough to smooth out this fiasco.

"This isn't personal. It's a business decision," Ed said. "Remember when we featured Gertie and Courtney in that series of ads for the moisturizing lotion. Sales shot through the roof."

How could Caleb forget? That campaign's success had floored everyone, including himself, and driven the company's brand recognition to new highs. Profits, too. "One in five women in the United States has tried a Fair Face product. You think we can achieve the same results here?"

"I do," Ed said. "As Bachelor of the Year you'll be the Grand Marshal of parades, do interviews and cut ribbons at grand openings. By the time we milk the last drop out of your title, two in five moms will be using our new products on their babies."

"Those numbers would make you happy," Glen said.

"I'd be thrilled." And Caleb would be.

He thought about the numbers. The exposure. The profits.

Face it. The website contest wasn't that big a deal in the grand scheme of things. One date. With a stranger. No big commitment.

Except for Becca.

Becca.

What was he worried about?

He liked her. They weren't exactly dating. They had fun together. Getting seriously involved with her would be too complicated and only add to his list of responsibilities. Becca. Her parents, Debbie and Rob. All the dogs.

That would be too much with everything else on Caleb's plate.

This Bachelor of the Year award would be the perfect reason for him to refocus on work and get Becca out of his heart—make that head. He was blowing a few dates—uh, get-togethers—out of proportion. He wasn't about to fall in love with her.

No worries at all.

Besides, Becca was one of the most practical women he knew. She would understand that he was doing this for Fair Face. She wouldn't care.

At least she shouldn't.

They weren't boyfriend and girlfriend. They hadn't made any type of commitment to one another. He wasn't going down that path again any time soon. If ever.

"Okay," Caleb said. "Let's make this work."

CHAPTER TWELVE

AT AN ITALIAN café in downtown Boise, Becca sat across from Caleb. "Thanks for inviting me out to dinner tonight. I didn't expect this at all."

"I'm glad you didn't have other plans."

She couldn't think of a better way to spend a Friday evening. "Well, I must admit it was a tough choice. Going out to dinner with you or getting ready for the dog show tomorrow."

He glanced up from his menu. "I'm honored you picked me."

Her heartstrings played a romantic tune that matched the violin music playing in the restaurant.

Romantic, indeed, with a lit candle stuck into a wax covered bottle of Chianti. A single red rosebud sat in a small glass vase, looking so perfect she'd wondered if the flower were real. One sniff of the sweet fragrance answered that question.

Real.

Just like tonight.

Becca looked over her menu at Caleb. He wore a navy suit, white button-down collared shirt and a colorful red tie with swirly patterns.

Proper CEO, definitely.

Handsome, oh yes. Swoonworthy, no doubt.

Becca swallowed a sigh. She liked spending time with him. It didn't matter what they did, either. His company and his kisses were more than enough. A good thing he seemed to agree.

She'd worried what happened at the hospital with Courtney had changed things between them. He hadn't called or texted. But Becca knew he had to be busy like her. "I wanted you to know Courtney is working on the labels for the dog products. She has an eye for design."

"Wait until you see the finished product."

"Caleb…"

"Okay, that wasn't nice of me." He looked over the top of his menu. "You'll be happy to know Courtney's going to be doing four-week rotations through various departments to see what type of jobs are available at Fair Face."

"That's wonderful."

"We'll see how it goes."

"Have faith."

"You haven't been through this with Courtney before."

"No, but I've been through it," Becca said. "Imagine if Gertie hadn't taken a chance on me. We wouldn't be here to-night."

The thought sent a chill down her spine. Becca expected Caleb to say something funny or sincere. She wanted him to smile or laugh. Instead he returned to reading his menu.

That was…odd. Maybe he'd had a rough day at the office. "Good day at work?"

"Typical."

His one-word answer was atypical. Usually he told her about something he'd done, a story from a meeting or an office anec-dote. She wondered if something had happened that he didn't want to talk about.

"Know what you're going to order?" she asked.

He perused the menu. "The salmon looks good. You?"

"The halibut special sounds tasty."

"It does."

Standard dinner conversation, except it wasn't standard for them. Each word made her want to squirm in her seat. Maybe she was being paranoid. Overly analytical. Or maybe some-thing was really going on.

She crinkled the edges of the menu. The words blurred. She couldn't stand it. "Is something wrong?"

"I wouldn't say wrong."

Okay, she wasn't paranoid. But that didn't make the churning of her stomach any better.

"What's going on?" Becca tried to sound nonchalant. She wasn't sure if she succeeded. She took a sip of water, hoping to wash away the lump in her throat.

"I was named Boise's Bachelor of the Year today."

Becca choked on the water in her mouth, coughed, but managed not to spit the liquid out. She swallowed instead.

"Wow." She tried to think of something to say other than *But aren't you going out with me?* "You must be...excited."

"I wouldn't say excited."

That made her feel a little better. She bit the inside of her cheek. "So this isn't that big a deal?"

He set his menu on the table. "Everyone at Fair Face is calling it a PR coup."

"A coup?"

"I'm being interviewed on *Good Day Boise* next week."

"Wow." Oops. She'd already said that. But her mind was reeling. "A TV interview is huge."

"I've done interviews before."

Caleb was downplaying this. Maybe Bachelor of Year was like the Sexiest Man Alive award, more of an honorary title than anything else. No reason for her to freak out. They might be dating, but technically he was still a bachelor.

Becca needed to be supportive, not act like a shrew. She raised her glass in the air. "Congrats."

He studied her with an odd expression. "You don't...mind."

"Why would I mind?" She asked the question as much for her benefit as his. "I don't see a ring on your finger."

Or one on hers.

But even though she knew better, even though his harsh words at the hospital had stung, she could imagine a tuxedo-clad Caleb sliding a shiny gold wedding band on her finger.

Her insides twisted. She took another sip of water. It didn't help.

He picked up his menu. "Thanks for being so understanding about this."

"Why wouldn't I be understanding?" She asked herself aloud. "It's an honor."

"You're really great, you know that."

So that was what being understanding got her. She would take it. "Thanks. Though I have no doubt women are going to be throwing themselves at you wanting to capture the Bachelor of the Year's heart."

His smile returned, reaching all the way to his eyes. "They can try, but they won't succeed."

Caleb's words put her at ease. His heart wasn't up for grabs because it was spoken for...by her. Even Becca's fingernails felt as if they were smiling. "Good to know."

"Don't worry about any of this," he said. "It'll be a big infomercial for Fair Face's new organic baby product line."

"Bachelor and babies. Not the usual combination."

"It's how things are done these days."

Business, she reminded herself. Nothing personal. How many times had she heard that since meeting Caleb?

More times than she could remember. Except...

Something niggled at her. Something she couldn't quite explain.

The feeling was familiar, like a little voice of caution whispering inside her head. The voice she should have listened to before going out with Whit and his friends that fateful night.

Crazy. She was thinking crazy thoughts now. Going overboard with the paranoia.

Caleb Fairchild was nothing like those rich kids back in high school. He might wear designer labels, drive an expensive car and have a ton of money, but he cared about her.

Everything he'd done, everything he was doing, proved that.

Maybe he hadn't fallen for her as she'd fallen for him. But he liked her. She should enjoy this time with Caleb, not borrow trouble. Things would only get better between them. A satisfied smile settled on her lips.

"You look happy," he said.

"I am."

"You've put me in a much better mood."

That pleased her. "Being with you makes me happy."

"I want you to be happy."

Becca's heart sang with joy. He did care. She knew it.

Ever since Caleb had entered her life, things had gotten better, not worse. The words *I love you* sat on the tip of her tongue. They would be so easy to say.

But she wanted the timing to be right. She wanted the place to be perfect. She wanted him to say the words back to her.

Becca needed to wait. Just a little while. Let this bachelor thing blow over. Give them more time to make memories together.

But soon. Very, very soon.

Tuesday morning at the television studio, the lights beat down on Caleb. Sweat streamed down his back, a mix of heat and nerves.

The red light on the two cameras reminded him the show was being shown live. He needed to at least act like he'd rather be here than at the dentist for a root canal.

But sitting on the couch with Savannah and Thad, the hosts of *Good Day Boise*, was the height of awkwardness. The two looked like pictures from a plastic surgeon's office with their bleached smiles, pouty fish lips and straight, proportioned noses. They droned on about this year's bachelor candidates and why Caleb had been chosen number one.

He kept a smile super-glued on his face and nodded when he thought appropriate.

Savannah leaned toward him with a coquettish grin. The V-neckline of her dress gaped, showing her cleavage. Caleb looked away.

Thad laughed, though Caleb had no idea at what. "The big questions our female viewers want to know—"

"Single female viewers," Savannah interrupted. "Though there may be a couple married ones, too."

Thad guffawed. Or maybe it was another of his fake laughs. "Is there a special woman in your life, Caleb?"

Becca. An image of her appeared front and center in his mind. Her sweet smile made his day. Her beautiful eyes lit up each time she saw him. Her hot kisses turned him on. She was special, more special than any other woman he'd dated.

Saying Becca's name would be easy. Saying Becca's name felt right. Saying Becca's name wasn't part of the script he was supposed to follow.

It didn't matter anyway. She understood. She'd said so herself on Friday night. She wouldn't care or be upset. They weren't serious.

Caleb took a deep breath. "No one special. Which is too bad."

"Why is that?" Thad asked.

The hosts gobbled the bait, exactly the way Ed had said they would. Time to reel them in with the money shot. Or in this case the perfect sound bite. Caleb straightened. "Because I want to start a family."

Savannah and Thad exchanged glances. Excitement danced in their eyes. "Boise's Bachelor of the Year wants a family?"

They spoke in unison, in a creepy kind of singsong voice.

The image of Becca remained front and center in mind, calling to Caleb.

Speak up, his heart cried.

Why the hell was his heart involved in this? It shouldn't be. No woman could touch his heart. Not even...

Get with the program, Fairchild.

Caleb swallowed around the lump in his throat. He pushed the image of Becca from his mind. He needed to follow the script. "Yes, I want a family. Having one is important to me."

Savannah touched his sleeve with her bright red painted

nails, making him think of a spider, the kind who eats their mates. "What is a handsome, rich industrialist looking for in his perfect woman?"

Perfect woman.

The two words made his stomach turn.

Caleb knew what he wanted. Who he wanted. But the PR department had dreamed up a list for him. A list that technically fit his position and roughly reflected his interests for a woman who Caleb would have, up to this point, considered an ideal spouse. "Educated, a keen sense of humor, stylish, fit, well-traveled, social, a little sophisticated, a foodie, a discriminating ear when it comes to music and plays tennis."

Each word rang hollow.

Such a woman was safe, dull, orderly.

Like his life.

Becca was so much more than the sum of all those items on the list. Fun, energetic, nurturing.

He wanted to tell the hosts and the audience about Becca, about her amazing qualities. But Fair Face was counting on him. It didn't matter what he thought. It didn't matter what he wanted.

Ty was downrange fighting bad guys to keep their country safe. Caleb was stuck on a couch lying his ass off because safe and dull had made his family company successful.

"Sounds like there might be a woman or two in Boise who share some of those characteristics," Savannah said.

Yes, but he wanted only one woman.

No, he didn't.

Caleb was getting in too deep. The fact that Becca kept coming up told him that. He'd lowered his guard too much and let her into his heart. Bad move. He couldn't trust romantic relationships. Being involved in a serious relationship was too difficult. Too much work and responsibility. He'd had enough of that already. "I hope so."

Except being with Becca hadn't been work, his heart countered. She made him happy.

He wanted his heart to shut up.

He'd tried getting married. That relationship had been a disaster. Becca wasn't trying to scam him. As special as she was, as much as she hadn't been a burden, he didn't want to fall in love with her. He couldn't do that to himself. Or her.

Caleb had gotten too close to her, too fast. He needed to pull back, stop seeing her, focus on Fair Face.

The expectations of the marketing and PR departments were riding on Caleb's every word, weighing him down and making him sweat. He always did what was expected of him. This was no different.

Stick with the script.

"I'd hate to think I'd never be able to use Fair Face's new line of organic baby products on my own children."

Savannah sighed along with the audience full of smiling women. "Baby products."

He'd elicited the right response from her and the audience. Good, except his victory felt empty.

"My grandmother's ready to be a great-grandmother. She created the products as a not-so-subtle hint to me. All I'm missing is…"

"A wife," Savannah said with glee.

"Perhaps we can help you find her," Thad said.

Savannah nodded enthusiastically. "We're going to hold a contest on our website to find Boise's Bachelor of the Year's perfect woman."

"She could be sitting in our studio audience. Or maybe she's watching at home," Thad said. "Go to our website and find out if you have the qualities to be Caleb's perfect woman. The prize is a dream date with Boise's Bachelor of the Year. Who knows? The date could turn into something more!"

"Thanks." The word felt as if Caleb was eating tar. "I could use all the help I can get finding her!"

One thought ran through Caleb's head. Too bad he couldn't have been voted the second most eligible bachelor in Boise this year.

At least this would be over soon. He would go on the stupid date, then get on with his life. Alone, the way he liked it.

Win-win, right?

Becca stared at the television set in the guest cottage. She held on to two dogs, Dozer and Hunter, one on each side of her. Each breath took concerted effort. Her throat burned. Tears filled her eyes.

Don't cry. Don't cry. Do not cry.

She blinked back the tears.

She'd set the DVR to record the interview. She never wanted to watch it again. Not ever.

Her heart ached, a painful, squeezing kind of hurt. Disappointment. Betrayal.

Caleb had made her think this bachelor-of-the-year thing was no big deal. That it was business.

PR opportunity or not, his words on this morning's interview stung. More than she ever thought possible.

So much for protecting her heart.

Becca hadn't. It had splintered into a million razor sharp shards. And now…

Women all over Boise, likely northern Idaho and eastern Oregon, were going to be vying to be Caleb's perfect woman and go on a dream date with him in hopes of being his wife.

Thank goodness she hadn't told him she loved him.

She wanted to throw up.

It was clear she wasn't his perfect woman.

Tears continued to sting her eyes.

Judging by the list of qualities, he was looking for a woman with a similar background and upbringing. She might be able to write a business report, but an AA degree didn't count as educated. Preferring hot dogs to fancy food meant she couldn't call herself a foodie. She'd never travelled outside the Pacific Northwest.

Hurt sliced through her stomach. All her insecurities rushed to the surface.

The dogs squirmed out of her arms. She let them go.

Why had Gertie played matchmaker when Becca was so wrong for Caleb?

Becca wrapped her arms around her stomach.

Gertie should never have chosen some fish out of water to put in the rich, corporate aquarium for her grandson. Dating might not influence Fair Face's bottom line, but there was intrinsic value to the woman Caleb…married.

Becca rocked back and forth.

Caleb had shown his practical side during the interview. He didn't need someone who preferred the company of dogs, not dressing up and eating hot dogs. He needed a corporate wife. Someone who could entertain, dress the part and play hostess. A trophy wife.

The vise tightened around Becca's heart, pressing and squeezing out the blood. She sniffled.

How had she completely misread the man? Maybe she'd ignored signs because she enjoyed being with him. The same way she'd ignored the signs with Whit.

It hadn't felt the same, but she could have been fooling herself. She had to have been fooling herself.

Caleb hadn't told her about the dream date contest, only being named Bachelor of the Year and doing an interview. He'd lied by omission, making her wonder if he'd lied about other things. Lied or…been practical?

She'd told him she wouldn't pretend to be someone she wasn't after what happened with Whit. If she wasn't what Caleb wanted, was this his way of breaking up with her?

Becca couldn't answer that question herself, but she intended to find out the answer.

If not for the time of day, champagne would have been flowing at Fair Face. Interest in the new baby line had skyrocketed following Caleb's interview. Whatever issues he'd had about saying he wanted to settle down had disappeared.

Genius. Brilliant. Smart move.

The words described how wonderfully they'd pulled off the PR coup on *Good Day Boise*. There was only one loose end to tie up, and he could relax.

Becca.

His assistant buzzed him. "Ms. Taylor is here to see you."

Okay, that was weird. He hadn't expected her to come to him. But he might as well get this over quickly so he could attend the celebration in the company's cafeteria in honor of his award and interview. "Send her in."

Becca entered his office. She was dressed casually in a pair of plain khakis, a blue blouse and canvas tennis shoes. She looked neat, fit and very pretty. But she wasn't smiling

He didn't blame her.

As she walked in, the others in his office walked out.

"See you in the cafeteria," Ed said.

Caleb nodded. "Be down shortly."

The door closed. He walked around to the front of his desk and leaned against it. "You saw the interview."

"I did." She raised her chin. "I'm sure the show's servers are going to overload with all the women wanting to win a dream date with you."

Her sarcastic tone matched the expression on her face. "It's a contest. A promotion."

She pursed her lips. "Then why didn't you tell me about it?"

"I didn't think it mattered. It's just business."

"Business?" Disbelief filled her voice. "You listed all the qualities you're looking for in the perfect woman. None of which I have."

"The PR department provided the list. It was a publicity stunt. Nothing more."

"It hurt hearing you say all those things you were looking for and imagining the perfect corporate trophy wife who fits the list. A woman who wasn't me."

"I told you it wasn't my list," he said. "But it's not like we're seriously dating."

"Ouch." She stared at him as if he'd grown a third eye and horns. "At least I have bruises on both cheeks now."

"I never wanted to hurt you." But Caleb had, and he couldn't take it back.

Her bottom lip quivered.

It was all he could do not to take her in his arms so she would feel better. But he couldn't.

This was the best. For Becca and for him.

"So what happens next?" she asked. "And I don't mean your dream date. I'm talking about you and me."

You and me. Not us. That had to be a good sign. "I'm not in a place to have a serious relationship."

"I figured that much."

"You have a lot going on with the dog products and developing a handling career."

Her gaze narrowed. "Don't put any of this on me."

Guilt coated his throat. Okay, bad move. "It's me."

"Yes, it is." She wet her lips. "I want to know why you went out with me."

"Being with you was fun."

"Fun," she repeated twice. "I thought things were more serious than that."

"No. I can't. I'm sorry. I've been distracted. I need to get back to work."

"So this is about Fair Face?"

"After my father died, my grandparents' hopes and dreams for him were transferred onto me. I've spent my life trying to do everything my father didn't do. For my family and for Fair Face. I can't take anything else on."

"You mean me."

"Yes."

"I don't want to be your responsibility. I'm doing fine on my own."

Becca was. And she was cutting through his reasons like a skilled surgeon. He would try again.

"I'm not ready to make an emotional commitment." The

last time he did that it blew up in his face. Desire had a way of turning him inside out. He couldn't screw up again. "I can't risk the indulgence of a relationship right now."

Flames ignited in Becca's eyes. Her jaw tensed. "Indulgence of a relationship?"

"Perhaps that's the wrong word." He was bungling this up. He wasn't usually so clumsy and the hurt in Becca's eyes was killing him. He couldn't think straight. Not when she was around him. Even more proof he needed her out of his life. "I need to focus my attention on Fair Face. Nothing else. Not even the dog care products."

His words slammed into him, as if he'd punched himself in the gut. But he'd had no other choice than to say them. He couldn't keep seeing her.

Becca swallowed, but said nothing. Hurt dulled her eyes.

He reached for her, then drew his arm back. If he touched her, he might not want to let go. "Look, I could have gone about this differently. But I didn't. We had some good times together. Let's not have this blow up into something awful."

"That's the first thing you've said that I agree with." She met his gaze. "Thanks for opening my eyes to the truth."

"The truth?"

"You don't deserve me."

"Becca—"

"You act responsible and practical, but you're not." Her voice rose. "I'm guessing you went out with me to appease Gertie and keep her happy. You could make sure I wasn't trying to scam your grandmother and you could have a little fun at the same time."

"No." Her words hit him like a dagger to the heart. "I went out with you because I wanted to be with you. No other reason."

"But once things turned into something real, where you would have to take risk, you decided it was over between us. You could have spoken up, but that would have been too scary, so you followed someone else's script, the way you've done your entire life."

"That's not true." But his words didn't have a strong conviction behind them. He would try again. "Not true at all."

"It is true, because I was once there myself. But I'm over the wariness of my past. In part, thanks to you. But you're not because of your mother, your father and Cassandra. I'm not sure you ever will be, either." Squaring her shoulders, Becca met his gaze. "I never thought I'd say this, but I feel sorry for you, Caleb Fairchild."

She turned and walked to the door.

He stood, his heart pounding in his chest. "You have no idea what you're talking about."

Becca didn't glance back. She kept walking out of his office and out of his life.

Which was exactly what he'd wanted to happen.

So why did it hurt so badly?

CHAPTER THIRTEEN

BECCA FOUGHT THE urge to run out of Caleb's office. She made a conscious effort not to slam the door to his office behind her. She wasn't going to make a scene.

Or cry.

Her anger spiraled.

She knew her worth. She wasn't going to forget that or become someone else to make Caleb love her.

Screw him.

Becca should have seen through his BS, through the sweet words and tender smiles and hot kisses. Caleb couldn't accept her for who she was. He wanted someone more suited to his world. He wasn't willing to take a risk on her.

On them.

She marched to the elevator.

Caleb could blame his job at Fair Face or his family or a hundred other things, but bottom line…he wasn't capable of loving her as she was.

That was what Becca deserved.

What she wanted.

The elevator dinged. The doors opened.

Becca stepped inside. She poked the button for the lobby, nearly breaking one of her already short fingernails.

How could she have been so stupid again?

She'd been trying to fit in and prove herself in order to gain Caleb's acceptance. But the people who truly loved her and knew her accepted her fully, the way the dogs did. People like Gertie and her parents. Anything Becca accomplished was the proverbial icing on the cake.

She hadn't needed to earn their love.

Love was unconditional. And if it wasn't, she wasn't interested. Period.

The weeks ran into each other. Caleb tried to focus on work, but thinking about Becca distracted him as much as when she was a part of his life. He kept telling himself things had worked out for the best. Breaking it off now had saved them both from suffering any real hurt. It was time to move on.

But tonight, on his dream date at Pacifica, he had to wonder if moving on had been for the best.

Sweat dripped down the back of Caleb's neck due to the heat of the camera light and nerves.

A cameraman stood next to the table for two, filming every moment Caleb spent with a beautiful blonde thirty-year-old woman named Madeline Stevens. He had to give the matchmaker credit. Madeline met all the PR department's qualifications and then some. She'd graduated from Yale, studied in Paris and owned an art gallery. She sat on the board of two local nonprofits. She had a centerfold-worthy body and wore a sexy little black cocktail dress that showed off her curves. She was everything a man in his position should want in a girlfriend, a wife even.

Except she wasn't…Becca.

Madeline glanced at the camera. "I had no idea tonight would be a threesome."

Sense of humor, check. He'd been crossing off the qualities she met from his mental list. "No one mentioned we'd have a chaperone and everything would be on camera."

He would never have agreed to this if he'd known a follow-up story, complete with film footage, would be shown on *Good Day Boise*.

"Well, I guess we're getting a taste of what being on a reality TV show would be like," she said.

"I'll pass."

"Me, too." She stared up through her mascara-covered eyelashes at him and lowered her voice. "Maybe we can ditch him and find some place private where we can…talk."

The suggestive tone of her voice told him talking wasn't what she had in mind. But strangely, Caleb wasn't the least bit interested in doing anything other than calling it a night.

He didn't want Madeline to feel uncomfortable, though he sure did. He hated being here. Hated having to pretend to be interested in such a lovely woman when he'd rather be eating hot dogs at home by himself or peanuts with Becca.

The cameraman moved in closer, then adjusted the microphone.

Caleb needed to keep the conversation flowing, something he'd struggled to do with Madeline. Unlike with Becca. If she were here, the discussion would flow, uninterrupted, from topic to topic.

He didn't understand why he was out with a stunningly attractive woman and thinking about Becca, especially after what she'd said to him. But he couldn't get her out of his head. "So, do you have any pets?"

"No," Madeline said. "I work long hours. I don't think it would be fair to a dog or cat to leave them alone."

Good answer. One that Becca—make that Grams—would approve of. "I don't have any pets or plants for the same reason."

She leaned forward. Her face puckered in distaste. "There are silk plants. But at least live plants don't shed dog hair."

Caleb remembered Maurice and Becca's lint roller. "My grandmother has a couple of dogs that leave hair everywhere. It's not that bad. Unless you're wearing black."

Madeline's eyes narrowed. She wet her lips. "Oh, no. I never meant that it was bad. I'm an animal lover. Dogs are the sweetest things. One of these days, I'll adopt one from a rescue group."

Her backtracking reminded him of Cassandra, who'd said whatever she thought he wanted to hear. The total opposite of Becca, who spoke her mind, whether he wanted to hear it or not.

He remembered being at the dog show with her. "Dogs are a lot of work."

"That's why people use doggy day cares."

The words made him cringe. Becca would never take a dog to a place like that. She would rather care for them herself.

The way she'd taken care of Grams's dogs and Grams and Courtney and…

Him.

His mouth went dry. He picked up his water glass and drank. It didn't help. He took another sip. The funny feeling in the pit of his stomach only worsened.

What had he done?

He'd been so worried about taking on one more responsibility, but he shouldn't have been. Becca had been taking care of all of them, especially him, from the day he met her.

He'd been wrong about her past.

He was wrong about her.

But he couldn't see that until sitting here with a woman who on paper should have been perfect for him, but wasn't.

Not Madeline's fault. She was too much like Cassandra and totally different from…

Becca.

Tomorrow he would go to her. Apologize. Ask for a second chance.

All he had to do was survive the camera and the rest of his dream date. He hoped that the rest of the evening didn't turn into a nightmare.

The next morning Caleb arrived at the estate and rang the doorbell.

Mrs. Harrison opened the door. "Your grandmother is in her bedroom."

"What about Becca?"

"I believe she's on her way to a dog show."

Damn. That would complicate talking with her. He entered Grams's room to find her packing. "Where are you going?"

"Enumclaw, Washington." She folded a pink T-shirt. "Big dog show. We have a vendor booth for our products."

"Is Becca going to be there?"

"She left yesterday in the RV with the dogs and her parents. I'm meeting her there later today." Grams stopped packing. "How was your dream date last night? Did you find your perfect woman?"

The sarcasm in Grams's voice was clear. Caleb took a deep breath. "I won't be asking the winner out again, if that's what you're asking."

"At least you haven't lost all your brain cells." Grams returned to packing. "Before I forget, I need you to schedule a week's vacation. I'll give a range of dates to your assistant before I head out."

"Why?"

"Your birthday present."

"My birthday isn't until January."

"With your schedule, I need to plan ahead."

"Where am I going?"

"A navy SEAL training camp."

His heart skipped two beats. He could barely breathe. He'd always wanted to attend one. He had the money, but not the time. He'd also never told anyone he wanted to go, not even Ty. "How did you…?"

"I buy your gift in the summer, since your birthday is close to Christmas. That way I make sure it's different. Special."

"But SEAL training?" he forced the question from his dry throat.

"Becca. It was her idea, " Grams said. "I wasn't sure about it."

"It's the perfect gift."

"That's what Becca said."

Becca.

Of course she would be the one to suggest the gift. She knew him, really and truly knew him.

And she was exactly the woman he needed.

He'd been such a fool. An idiot.

I learned my lesson. I'm not going to try to be someone I'm not ever again.

No wonder hearing that list had hurt Becca so much. Caleb had known what she'd gone through with Whit, but he'd been thinking only about Fair Face and himself. Not how hearing the list of his perfect qualifications would affect and hurt Becca. She was correct, he didn't deserve her.

But he loved her. He wanted her back.

His chest tightened with regret.

Becca was the one for him.

He should have screamed her name during his interview, not gone along with someone else's script for his life and taken another woman on a dream date. He should have held on to Becca with both hands, not let her walk out of his office and out of his life. He should have told her she was his perfect woman, not let her think she wasn't.

"Grams…"

She walked to his side and touched his face. "You're pale as a ghost."

He was so used to taking care of everyone, but he hadn't taken care of Becca. Not the way she'd taken care of him. "I've made a big mistake. The biggest mistake of my life."

"With Becca?"

Caleb nodded. He had always done what was expected of him. He'd put his own dreams aside. He'd put his life on hold. He'd hurt someone he cared about because that was what everyone expected him to do.

No longer.

Becca had been right. He'd been following a script. That was easier than risking his heart only to be hurt again.

He was in the doghouse, but he was willing to beg, to perform tricks, to do whatever was needed to be a part of her life. She didn't need him. But he needed her. Her smile, her sense of humor, her love.

Grams smiled. "So how do you intend on fixing it?"

Becca walked out of Ring Five with Hunter's leash in one hand and a Best of Winners—the prize for a dog still working on his championship ribbon—in the other. The sun beat down, but the beagle didn't seem to mind. She couldn't wait to remove her suit jacket.

Gertie stood, her hands clasped together and a bright smile on her face.

Becca handed off the ribbon. "He needs one more major and he's a champion."

"So proud of both of you."

"Thanks." The word sounded flat. Becca couldn't help it. Normally she would be thrilled with the win, bouncing on her toes and tingling with excitement, but it was all she could do to keep her feet moving and not retreat to the RV to nap.

Maybe some caffeine would help. She'd been living off coffee lately.

Heaven knew she needed something to get her out of this funk. She couldn't quite shake her sadness. She'd tried pushing Caleb out of her thoughts. She'd succeeded somewhat, but she couldn't get him out of her heart.

At least not yet.

The feeling would pass. Someday. Someday soon she hoped.

But she was better off having met Caleb. He'd shown her what she wanted and didn't want.

"Let's go see how your parents are doing at the booth." Gertie had hired Becca's parents to sell the products at dog shows and fill online orders. "I also want to show off Hunter's ribbon."

They walked along the row of vendor booths, tables and displays set up under pop-up canopies that provided shade.

"Your parents have company at the booth," Gertie said.

Becca was pleased by how much her parents enjoyed talking to dog owners about the products. Gertie called them "natural salespeople." Maybe so, but Becca also knew they were friendly hard workers who didn't want to disappoint Gertie or their daughter. "Customers are a good thing."

"I don't think this one is interested in dog products."

Becca looked over and froze.

Caleb.

Her heart tumbled. She couldn't breathe.

"What's he doing here?" she asked, her voice shaking as much as her insides.

"Let's find out."

"No." Becca's feet were rooted to the pavement. She couldn't have moved. Even if she were being chased by vampires or brain-eating zombies or ax-wielding murderers, she would be eaten or slain where she stood. "You go."

She stared at him in his khakis and polo shirt. She could only see his backside, but every nerve ending tingled as if she'd touched a live wire and sent a jolt of electricity through her.

Gertie pulled on Becca's arm. "Come on. You're no coward."

"Yes, I am."

Gertie gave a not-so-gentle shove. "Chin up and move those feet, girlie."

Becca moved. It was either that or fall over. With each step, an imaginary boom, like a timpani, echoed through her. "I can't—"

"Yes, you can," Gertie encouraged. "One step in front of the other."

Becca crossed the aisle toward their booth. Lightheaded and stomach churning, she thought passing out was a distinct possibility. At least in that case, she wouldn't have to face him.

"Caleb," Gertie said.

He turned. Smiled.

Becca went numb.

"Hello," he said, as if his being at a dog show in a different state was to be expected.

She opened her mouth to speak, but no words came out.

He looked at Becca with warm, clear eyes. "I missed you."

Her heart slammed against her ribs. Anger surged. "Is this some kind of joke?"

"No joke." Caleb motioned to the booth. "Looks like the products are selling thanks to your top-notch sales force."

Becca's parents smiled at her.

She stared at Caleb, her temper spiraling out of control. "You discard me like garbage. Hurt my feelings worse than anyone, which is saying a lot. Then show up here as if nothing had happened. Unbelievable."

Tension sizzled in the air. People glanced her way, but kept walking. Two dogs barked at each other.

"You're right." He sounded contrite, but that didn't make her feel any better. "You've always been right."

Okay, she hadn't been expecting that.

"I am here. I don't blame you if you don't want to talk to me, but I hope you'll hear me out."

A beat passed. And another. "Five minutes."

He pulled her to one side and glanced at his watch. "I was getting too attached to you. I was distracted at work. I was happier with you than my own family. That scared me. You scared me. I was too afraid to take a risk. Too afraid you might be the one to break me. So I played it safe. Too safe. And I lost the one person I need most in my life. The one person who understands me. The one person who makes me stronger. You took care of me in a way no one else had. I miss that. I miss you."

The air rushed from her lungs. A lump burned in her throat. Tears stung her eyes. She couldn't think. She couldn't speak.

"You're amazing, unique and everything I didn't realize I wanted until you came into my life, and then I stupidly let you go," he continued. "I'm sorry for the crappy way I treated you. I was no better than that idiot Whit. But I apologize. For doing the asinine interview and agreeing to the contest. For not telling you and then breaking up the way that I did. I don't blame you for not loving me after all I've done, but I love you. And if there's any way you could find it in your heart to forgive me, I'll make it up to you. I want to spend the rest of my life making it up to you."

She forced herself to breathe. "That's why you came here?"

He nodded. "I was going to go crazy if I had to spend another day without seeing you."

Her heart melted. She knew better, but it didn't matter.

"I think I have at least another two minutes. Maybe three." His eyes were earnest, his voice sincere. "Do I stand a chance?"

She wanted to say no. She wanted to tell him to go. She wanted to move on without him.

His smile practically caressed her.

But her heart wanted something different. Wanted him.

"For as long as I can remember I've been trying to prove myself. If I did that, then I thought I could be accepted." Becca took a deep breath. "But Gertie encouraged me. Then you. I realized I didn't have to do anything special. I had to accept who I was and the rest would happen."

"It's happening."

Becca could feel it. Acceptance. Joy. Love.

"I forgive you." The way she'd finally forgiven herself for her past mistakes. "I'm ready to try a relationship, but I want the man beneath the pinstripes. The guy who grew up wanting to be a navy SEAL."

"He's yours." Caleb kissed her forehead. "But I don't want to try anything. I know the right woman, the perfect woman, for me."

He dropped down on one knee.

Becca gasped.

Caleb held her hand. "Will you marry me, Becca? Be my wife and partner and dog whisperer?"

Maurice trotted toward Becca. Her father held one end of the long leash. The dog came closer. A white ribbon was tied to his collar. Hanging from the ribbon was a…ring.

Her throat tightened. "You're serious."

Caleb nodded. "I asked your dad's permission."

Based on her parents' beaming faces, Caleb had no doubt received approval and been offered help with the proposal.

"So what do you say?" he said.

"I come with baggage."

"You also come with lint brushes," he said. "A fair trade-off in my book."

That was all she needed to hear. Know.

"Yes." Happiness flowed through her. "Yes, I'll marry you."

He removed the ring from Maurice's collar. The entire gold band was inlaid with tiny diamonds. In the center were bigger diamonds in the shape of a dog's paw. "I thought a large diamond would get in the way of all the things you have to do with the dogs. If you'd rather have—"

"This is perfect. I can't tell you how perfect."

He slid the ring onto her finger. "I love you."

"I love you."

He kissed her gently on the lips.

Maurice barked.

"Think he's jealous?" Caleb asked.

She glanced at the sparkling ring, then back at him. "No, that's his bark of approval."

"Let's give him more to approve of."

Caleb lowered his mouth to hers and kissed her. Hard.

Joy flowed through Becca, from the top of her head to the tip of her toes. The Boise Bachelor of the Year was off the market and would be ineligible to win ever again. But his kiss definitely deserved the prize for Best in Show. The first of many.

* * * * *